Praise for

PICTURES OF THE SHARK

Pictures of the Shark is a profound meditation on the limits of familial love and the uncontrollable forces that shape a man's heart. In these gorgeously crafted interlinked stories, Thomas H. McNeely demonstrates once again an uncanny ability to illuminate the darkest emotional corners of his characters with a vision that is as tender and compassionate as it is unflinching.

—**Antonio Ruiz-Camacho,** author of
Barefoot Dogs

McNeely's brilliant stories are filled with delicious menace and heartbreaking hope. The characters in McNeely's stories are terrified of the unknown, even as they suspect they know more than they should—about a father's lies, his other women, a mother's desperate yearnings, the perils of alcohol, and the terrifying bonds of love.

—**Pamela Painter,** author of
*What If? Writing Exercises
for Fiction Writers* and
*Fabrications: New and
Selected Stories*

This extraordinarily powerful novel-in-stories takes Philip Larkin's famous dictum—"They fuck you up, your mum and dad / They may not mean to, but they do"—and brings it to harrowing life. In prose as clear and flawless as the Texas sky, McNeely paints an indelible portrait of emotional harm, following
Buddy's journey from an innocent boy trapped in the fallout of a toxic marriage, to an alcoholic artist-in-love, to a damaged man who finds he will "always be his father's son." The story "Tickle Torture," alone, is worth the price of this book. McNeely is one of the least gimmicky, most emotionally insightful writers around, and *Pictures of the Shark* sneaks up on you, stealthily, to devastating effect.

—**Eric Puchner,** author of
Last Day on Earth and
Model Home

With masterful prose, McNeely draws you down into emotional depths where your ambivalence and confusion show you at your most profoundly human. These stories hook you quickly and deeply and keep you even after they end.

—**C.W. Smith,** author of
Steplings, Buffalo Nickel, and
Understanding Women

A linked collection that resembles *Jesus' Son* by Denis Johnson . . . but McNeely's protagonist tries to know himself by facing his shadow side. We watch him, wounded by his father's narcissism and neglect, grow into a man who knows he has similar faults. He can't distinguish between what is real and what he desires. He's a writer searching for truth but creating in order to lose himself. He claims to practice negative capability but lapses into the same dark patterns. *Pictures of the Shark* is the profound and engaging study of a man who looks deeply into himself but is unable to resist the pull of fate.

—**Nan Cuba**, author of *Body and Bread*

A beautifully crafted collection of urban Texas stories. . . . The focus on loss, obsession, illusion, and compulsion opens up to a wider if also painful world when the alcoholic male protagonist is seen through a college girlfriend's perspective as she acknowledges his emotional abuse of her. . . . The last story seems to offer a kind of hope . . . as he glimpses that "it had"—whatever exactly "*it*" is to him just then—"nothing to do with me."

—**Elizabeth Harris**, author of
The Ant Generator and
Mayhem: Three Lives of a Woman

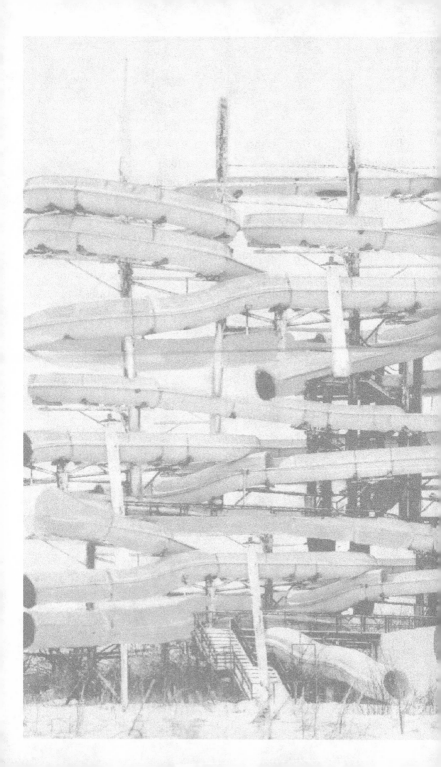

P[ICTURES OF TH]E SHARK

stories

THOMAS H. MCNEELY

★**trp**

The University Press of SHSU

Huntsville, Texas

www.texasreviewpress.org

Names: McNeely, Thomas H., author
Title: Pictures of the shark : stories / Thomas H. McNeely. Description:
Huntsville, Texas : Texas Review Press, [2022] Identifiers: LCCN 2021045665
(print)
LCCN 2021045666 (ebook)
ISBN 9781680032710 (paperback)
ISBN 9781680032727 (ebook)
Subjects: LCGFT: Short stories.
Classification: LCC PS3613.C585948 P53 2022
(print) LCC PS3613.C585948 (ebook) DDC 813/.6—dc23
LC record available at https://lccn.loc.gov/2021045665
LC ebook record available at https://lccn.loc.gov/2021045666
Author Photo Credit: Isobel Farone
Photograph: Matthew Henry at Unsplash
Book design and cover art: PJ Carlisle

for Alice Mayra

Also by Thomas H. McNeely:

Ghost Horse (Gival Press)

CONTENTS

For the listener, who listens in the snow,
And, nothing himself, beholds
Nothing that is not there and the nothing that is.

—"The Snow Man," Wallace Stevens

How they awaited him, those little deaths!
They waited like sweethearts. They excited him.

—"The Rabbit Catcher," Sylvia Plath

Snow, Houston, 1974

Through the window next to his bed, Buddy watched his father build a wire cage to house a light bulb to keep the bougainvillea bush warm. The weatherman had warned it would get down to the twenties that night, a record low for Houston. As usual, Buddy's father had appeared after the ten o'clock news, and Buddy waited for him to pass beneath the back porch light, his white lab coat like a ghost. Now, his father knelt in the back yard, steam puffing out from the hood of his heavy jacket.

When Trip let himself in the back yard gate, offering to help, Buddy's father waved him away. By that time, a pink blanket glowed on the wire cage. Trip stood there a moment, hands in his pockets, then slipped up the steps outside Buddy's window. From the kitchen behind his bed came Trip's and his mother's muffled voices.

Buddy put on a jacket like his father's, leaving his feet bare. The bright yellow kitchen was filled with plants his mother had brought in. Trip leaned against the clothes dryer near the back door, grinning at him through his scraggly beard. Buddy's mother sat at a yellow table in the middle of the room.

"Where do you think you're going?" he asked Buddy.

"Outside," Buddy said.

Outside, the night air stung his face. Without turning to him, his father said, "What do you think?" admiring the pink lantern the blanket made.

"It'll catch fire," Buddy said.

His father glanced over his shoulder, but the hood of his jacket hid his face. "Is that right? How come you know everything?"

Buddy hadn't meant that. His toes felt like ice on the rough cement.

"You better go inside," his father said. "If you get sick, I'll have to fix you, too."

After his mother sent him to bed again, Buddy watched his father guard the blanket. When she'd asked if the light bulb would be all right, his father hadn't answered her.

During the week, his father worked at the hospital where his mother taught medical technology, and on weekends, he studied enormous books with tissue-thin pages. Most nights Trip, who used to be his mother's med tech student, but was now in medical school with Buddy's father, came to the kitchen to drink beer and talk. Often, Buddy watched them from the hallway near the kitchen. When Trip asked his mother when she was going back to medical school, she glanced at Buddy's father and said she was too old for such nonsense. "You're never too old to take chances," Trip said. Buddy's father let out a sharp bark, which was supposed to be a laugh, but made his mother jump. She told Trip she had Buddy and his father, which was everything she needed.

Some nights, his parents talked alone. Once, Buddy had seen his father put his face on his mother's shoulder and cry. He'd backed down the hallway, caught his heel on a nail, and hollered, afraid of what he'd seen. His parents had looked at him as if they did not quite know who he was.

When Buddy woke, the kitchen was silent. His father no longer stood outside. As Buddy watched, the blanket seemed to smolder; he swelled with pride and fear, because no one else was there to see it. Then, as if in a dream, flames leapt up. At the same time, Buddy's heart leapt, as if he'd wished the fire, to prove he was right.

"Fire!" he yelled. "Fire!"

A commotion arose in his parents' room. Through his window, Buddy saw his father rush down the back porch steps in his T-shirt and underwear to beat the blanket with a rolled-up newspaper. His mother came to sit on his bed. She thought he was afraid; he wasn't, though he pretended to be, to keep her there.

"Your poor father," she said.

Buddy must have fallen asleep, because the next thing he knew, his father stood in the doorway to his room. Above his white T-shirt, his father's face was dark. "Why didn't you tell me that was gonna happen?" he said to Buddy.

"It's not his fault," his mother said.

She hadn't caught the joke in his father's voice; she didn't know what Buddy had said. Now, it seemed like his and his father's secret, but Buddy didn't know what to say to let him know that he knew. Before he could answer, his father disappeared, calling his mother after him, and Buddy's face burned with shame at his own silence.

The morning was hushed and bright. On the roofs' mismatched shingles, on the stooped pecan tree, even in the steel fences' serried links, lay a thin, white dust Buddy had seen before only on TV. Around the bougainvillea, scraps of burnt blanket had turned gray with frost. He pulled his covers over his head and tried to decide if he should tell his father the snow was there.

Perhaps the snow would keep his father home.

He slipped out of bed, shivering when his feet touched the floor. The walls of his room were yellow and bare, its thin carpet the color of chewed gum. Until his father became a doctor, his mother said, they would have to be careful with what they bought at the grocery store, and how much heat they used at night. Some nights Buddy woke and sat up in bed, worried that he himself did not have a job.

At his parents' door, he stopped. His father had told him to knock, but he pushed it open, full of his surprise. Except for bookcases and his mother's picture of Robert Kennedy, the room was as dim and bare as his own. Blinds were drawn over the windows; two white lumps huddled

4

on the bed.

"It's snowing," Buddy said.

His father groaned, a sound that could be either serious or joking; now, it seemed serious. Before Buddy could retreat, his father bolted up, hair on end, as if he'd been shocked. "Why can't you knock on the goddamned door?" he said.

His mother peeked over the edge of the covers.

"It's snowing," Buddy said.

"It is not snowing," his father said. "It has never snowed in Houston, Texas."

His mother touched his father's arm.

"What you saw was not snow." His father's voice was slow and calm; it seemed less angry than before. "You wouldn't know snow if you saw it."

Buddy jumped onto the bed and shouted, "It's snow! It's snow! It's snow!"

Beneath him, his mother clutched the blanket to her chest. His father was yelling at him to get off the bed.

"Honey," his mother said. "Buddy, why don't you go back to sleep?"

On wobbly legs, he scrambled to the door and pulled it shut.

"I'm sorry, honey," his mother said.

"That's okay," his father said. "I need to get to the lab."

"What if he's right? Shouldn't we look?"

"You can look," his father said. "It doesn't matter to me."

Buddy started toward his room, then paused. Eyes stinging, he went to the kitchen. Careful not to upset the plants his mother had brought in, he carried a chair to the sink and stood on it. On a windowsill above the sink were seashells and bits of colored glass his mother looked at when she did the dishes. Outside, snow covered the ground more thickly; a car drove by, leaving a trail of faint stripes. Past the sloping telephone lines, low clouds swallowed the tall buildings downtown. In the window screen, snowflakes lodged, then quickly faded. Buddy gripped the windowsill and leaned across the sink, trying to glimpse them before they vanished.

"Buddy?" His mother stood next to him. The darkness of the room made the lines on her face deep and sharp, but her pale green eyes caught the soft window light.

"You're right," she said. "It's snow."

Buddy sat in the kitchen, watching TV. His mother had bundled him in a T-shirt, a regular shirt, a sweater, blue jeans, two pairs of socks, and his heavy jacket. The jacket, his father said, was actually two jackets in one; its bright orange lining could be turned inside-out when people wanted to be rescued, but its outer layer, the dull olive color of garbage bags, was camouflage. Buddy wore the camouflage.

While his mother dressed Buddy, the weatherman said that all schools would be closed that day. Buddy asked if his father was going to stay home, but his mother kept her lips drawn tight, her eyes focused on the buttons of his jacket. He thought of pale-faced Courtney Pensil, who played hide-and-seek with him at school. Sometimes Courtney cried when it was time to go home, because her father was mean, she said. His own father wasn't mean, his mother had told him, just frustrated.

Now, the weatherman pointed at a map where wispy clouds repeated their herky-jerky routes across the sky. He said it hadn't snowed in Houston since 1948, twenty-six years before. Twenty-six years was twenty more than Buddy had been alive. That it had snowed back then didn't surprise him; his parents made it sound as if strange and miraculous things had happened all the time. There was the bougainvillea bush, for example, which they planted when his mother had first bought the house, right after Buddy was born. Even his own birth, his mother told him, had been a kind of miracle. When Trip came over, they often recounted the story of Big Bertha, a machine in the lab that counted cells. One night, when Buddy's father was an intern, and his mother was still in medical school, Big Bertha had refused to function. Side-by-side, Buddy's parents, who were not then his parents, had counted cells all night with hand-held clickers, and that was how they had fallen in love. When they told the story, their voices became beautiful with mysterious words—hemoglobin, cytoplasm, platelets—that swam like brightly colored fish. In a picture from that time, his mother and father stood in front of Big Bertha, whose flat, gray face had a single glass porthole for an eye. His not-yet-parents smiled shyly, dressed in matching white lab coats. For a while, Buddy thought they had concocted him in Big Bertha, who winked in the background.

Now, his parents' voices came toward him from their room. Buddy covered his head with his jacket's fur-lined hood and secured its heavy brass zipper over his chin.

"You should be here studying," his mother said, entering the kitchen. "Or playing with Buddy. I'm not going in. That freeway's going to be treacherous."

"Someone has to do surgicals," his father said. "If it's me, they'll remember."

"What about Buddy?"

"Buddy," his father said. "Will you remember me when I'm gone?"

Buddy kept his eyes on the TV. His jacket felt hot, but he didn't dare take it off.

"Leave him out of this," his mother said; then her voice sank to a whisper. "Where are you going? Tell me the truth."

"I've told you," his father said. "That's enough."

His father's footsteps approached. Buddy gripped the sides of his chair. His father snatched the hood from his head.

His father's balding, oval head was very handsome. He smelled of aftershave, and his sparse hair was neatly combed. The knot of his tie and collar of his lab coat peeked out from beneath his jacket. Though his eyebrows were fierce, his eyes could be gentle. But now his face was rigid and flushed, his eyes two flat discs, like a doll's.

"What do you want me to do?" he said to Buddy.

"Leave him alone," his mother said.

Buddy said nothing; any answer might be the wrong one.

His father lowered the hood of Buddy's jacket over his eyes, so that Buddy was enclosed in darkness. Then he raised it, and Buddy saw him again. His father leaned sideways between Buddy and the TV; his eyes were gentle, his face kind and composed, as if the other face had never been.

"Earth to Buddy," he said.

Buddy couldn't help but grin.

"This jacket will keep you warm at thirty degrees below zero," his father said. "It's the same material that NASA uses to make space suits. Did you know that?"

Buddy shook his head.

"Are you going to have fun today?"

Buddy nodded.

"Would you like to do urinalysis and frozen sections instead?"

"No," Buddy said, grinning.

"Okay, then," his father said. "I'm gone."

While his mother finished crying and found a pair of gloves, Buddy went back and forth between the window and the TV, comparing views of the snow. Though his mother never cried when his father was there, she often did when he left. And there were many nights when his parents' voices in the kitchen became low, and Buddy went to the hallway, afraid that they were talking about how they would leave. On those nights, his mother asked his father where he had been, and his father explained that he'd been at the hospital, working for them.

Now, the weatherman reported gas fires and burst water mains and houses whose roofs had caved in. Some neighborhoods, he said, were without electricity or telephones. Buddy began to worry about Grandma Liddy.

Grandma Liddy and he made plans: to buy a cassette recorder with cigarette coupons, to write President Nixon and ask him why he lied, to build a miniature city out of matchboxes and toilet paper rolls. They had already started the city, chalking streets on the threadbare carpet in his mother's old room.

His mother came into the kitchen, wearing a trench coat and rain boots, a sweater and scarf over her regular clothes. She knelt in front of Buddy and pulled gloves onto his hands, keeping her eyes from his. "Can we go to Grandma Liddy's?" he said.

"No, honey. It's too dangerous to drive."

"We can walk."

"It's too far, honey. Besides, daddy might come home."

"So?"

"So he might wonder where we are."

Buddy looked down at her, seeking her eyes; he was sure that she was trying to trick him. "You should call Grandma Liddy," he said. "To make sure she's not frozen."

His mother bit her lip and said that he was right; she should call. She went back to the bedroom. When his father wasn't there, Grandma Liddy asked his mother where he was, and why she had married him. Now, his mother's voice sounded as it always did when she talked to Grandma Liddy: "I'm sorry, mother," she said. "I'm sorry."

On the TV were low houses blanketed with snow. Buddy wondered if one of them was Courtney's, and if her father was home.

When his mother opened the front door, the snow's whiteness took his breath. Through the window, he hadn't seen how bright it was. Yards and driveways, curbs and streets, were covered in a shining mantle. Buddy caught snowflakes on his glove and showed them to his mother.

"They're pretty," she said. But when he looked down, they were gone.

His mother held his hand. Their feet sank in the snow. The snow, invisible on his hand, fluttered onto the houses' steep roofs, darkening their squat, frowning, ochre-colored faces. Above him, the sky seemed heavy with brightness.

Buddy let go of his mother's hand and ran, stumbling, across the yard. He hoisted his hood over his head and zipped the front of his jacket over his face. Arms dangling in his sleeves, he moaned, "I'm a monster. I'm a hemogobblin."

Something plashed his back. Buddy turned, afraid that one of the older boys who lived across the street had snuck up. He unzipped his jacket enough to peek out. His mother smiled crookedly and threw another snowball at him.

Soon, they were running, dodging behind bushes, their shrieks absorbed in the thick, sharp air. His mother fell backward, waving her arms up and down in the snow. Afraid she was hurt, Buddy ran to her. Her pale green eyes gazed up at him, then past him, unblinking. Snow dotted her smooth, flushed cheeks, sparkled in her graying, teak-colored hair. Her expression was hopeful, as it was when she looked at the seashells and colored glass above the sink. He crouched next to her and put out his hand to wipe away the snow, but it had already faded.

"Lay down," she said. "Make a snow angel with me."

Snow crunched beneath his jacket, but he could not

feel its coldness. Above him, clouds passed so close he imagined he might touch them. He waved his arms. His mother said she remembered when it had snowed before. She'd been fifteen, and all she wanted was a little boy. "A boy just like you," she said.

"Does daddy remember?" he said.

"Probably not. He would've been three years old."

A strange, jealous pride lifted him; he was older than his father had been.

His mother told him to make a wish. Buddy asked her what she was wishing. "I can't tell," she said. "The angels won't deliver if you tell."

Buddy closed his eyes. The wish that his father would never come home brushed him like a hand in the dark. Shivering, he opened his eyes. Snow fell into them. His mother was pulling him up, saying they should make a snowman.

They rolled a mound of snow until it wouldn't budge, then stood and caught their breaths and began to roll another. His mother told the story of his birth. Each time she told it, it seemed different. Buddy never tired of hearing it. He asked her to repeat certain parts, like how he had come early and surprised her; or how the doctors had had to cut him out of her, and discovered that his eyes were opened in her womb.

But now she told a version he'd never heard before. Before he was born, before she'd even met his father, she had worked at the hospital, she said, and when she finally decided to go to medical school, she still had to work, because Grandma Liddy had no money to help her, even if she'd wanted to. "That's when I met your father at the lab," she said. "Sitting in those classes with a bunch of boys twelve years my junior was starting to make school seem as hopeless as Grandma Liddy had said it was. And I was tired all the time—so tired, Buddy, like my arms were cement and my eyelids were lead. I was thirty-three, and by the time your father showed up, I thought I would die alone."

They lifted the second ball and set it atop the larger one, then waited for it to fall apart. When it didn't, they knelt and began to roll another.

"Did you like Daddy?" Buddy asked, frightened by what she'd told him.

"Of course I did." Her glance flickered away. "I love him."

They placed a third snowball on the others and stepped back to view their work. The snowman teetered forward, as if battling a fierce wind. Buddy's mother told him to find branches for the snowman's arms, then went inside.

As he searched the yard, Buddy felt someone watching him. Afraid that it was the older boys, he steeled himself, and looked up.

Across the street, Trip waved at him from the Gages' front yard. He rented their garage apartment, where he had lived since he was his mother's student. Buddy looked down, pretending not to notice him. His father said that Trip still lived nearby because he was in love with Buddy's mother; his mother said she had never heard of anything so absurd. His father said that nothing was absurd. He asked whether Trip—the Tripster, his father called him— would have gone to medical school if he'd had a family to support. And what had the Tripster been up to, his father wanted to know, while he'd been busting his ass at the lab? Getting laid while his parents footed his college tuition? When Trip visited, his father stared at him as if Trip had a toy he coveted, and talked in a loud voice about college, though he and Trip hadn't gone to college together. Trip's laughter was polite and embarrassed, and it made Buddy blush with anger and shame.

His mother returned with a handful of leftover Halloween candy. The snowman's eyes became two green dots, his nose an orange triangle, his mouth a crooked red line. Above his eyes, Buddy's mother pressed pieces of licorice, which made the snowman's eyes look fierce, like his father's.

Buddy and his mother found two branches that ended in sharp prongs. Buddy wanted to strike the scheming smirk from the snowman's face, poke out his eyes, trample his snowy guts into the ground. As though she knew his thoughts, his mother took his branch and stuck it gently into the snowman's side. The snowman struggled, his smile desperate, and Buddy felt pity for him as strong as his anger had been.

"He's pretty sad-looking," his mother said.

"He looks like daddy."

"I know." His mother squinted past him. "Here comes Trip. Be nice."

From beneath his dark curls, which caught snowflakes like a garland, Trip watched them steadily. Unlike his father's eyes, Trip's were always the same, asking his mother a question that made her uncomfortable. He waved; Buddy's mother lifted her hand.

"Hey," Trip said. "I waved, but Buddy didn't see me."

"Buddy," his mother said.

"It's okay." Trip stopped, leaning close to his mother, who put her hands in her pockets. "Did Jimmy get that thing fixed last night?"

"He did," said Buddy's mother. "It worked just fine."

Why had his mother said that? Buddy thought. Though Trip couldn't see the bougainvillea now, because it was in the back yard, he would later. His mother's lie angered Buddy; it was stupid. Trip looked at the snowman, then at Buddy, his brown eyes sharp and foxy. "Did he help you with this?"

"No," Buddy said. "He's gone."

His mother cast him a silencing glance. "He's doing surgicals."

"Why's he doing that?" Trip smiled. "Surgery's canceled."

His mother stared at the grim-faced houses and white lawns. Buddy stood very still, afraid of what he'd done. "He's probably studying," she said.

Trip scuffed the ground. "You don't need this, Margot."

"I know what I need." His mother stood behind Buddy and rested her hands on his shoulders. "I don't want to discuss it right now."

"I'm sorry." Trip looked up at her, then at Buddy. "Want some company?"

His mother's grip tightened on Buddy's shoulders.

"We're fine."

"Maybe later?" Trip said.

"Maybe," said his mother. "When Jimmy gets home."

Buddy lay in bed, waiting for his father. Above the back yard, an oily haze ringed the moon. The snow made the fences shorter and the houses smaller. In the midst of the yard, the bougainvillea stood like a tangle of burnt-out wires. After Trip left, Buddy and his mother had gone to check on it. Usually, his parents spoke in wistful tones about the bougainvillea, as they did about Big Bertha, but now, when his mother touched its dark, sickly leaves, her voice frightened him. "Dead," she said. "This is what things look like when they're dead." The rest of the day, she had gone back and forth between the window and the TV. On the ten o' clock news were pictures of cars stuck in snow. She peered at them, her face close to the screen, her brow knit with worry. When President Nixon came on, she called him a lying creep, and seemed glad to be angry. The weatherman warned it would get down to the teens that night, another record low. When the news ended, she put Buddy to bed and made him promise not to listen when his father came home.

All day, Buddy had worried that his father might not come home because of his wish. At the dimmest edges of Buddy's memory, before his father began medical school, they had played long games of hide-and-go-seek. Nothing had been more delicious than the feeling of being hidden, of possibly having disappeared, except the joy of being found. Sometimes, his father went to answer the phone, or to help his mother in the kitchen, and Buddy, still hidden, listened to his own breathing, and wondered if he came out whether he would be invisible to his father, or whether he would have become a ghost.

Outside, his father's car roared, shuddered, was silent; then his dark, blurred figure rounded the corner of the house, his face hidden under the hood of his heavy jacket. He went to the bougainvillea, pinched a couple of its leaves, and climbed the back steps to the kitchen door. Under the porch light, his shadow slid across Buddy's bed.

From the kitchen, his parents' voices rumbled through his wall. Buddy slipped out of bed. The floor was cold, but not as cold as it had been that morning, and somehow this, more than anything else, impressed upon him the gravity of whatever was about to happen.

His father sat at the yellow table, staring at his hands. Buddy's mother leaned toward him, touching the sleeve of his lab coat. Her voice was soft and angry.

"All I'm asking is you tell me the truth. I don't even want to know her name. I will cook for you, clean for you, put food in our mouths, but I will not be lied to."

"I told you," his father said. "We had a rush on surgicals."

"There wasn't any surgery."

His father's cheeks flushed a deep, bloody red.

"I talked to Trip. Then I called the hospital to make sure."

"That poor son of a bitch." His father slowly shook his head, staring at the table. "Don't you know he's so jealous of me he can't see straight? He's been trying to get you into bed for five years now, and as far as I know, it hasn't worked. They're gonna kick him out of the program—Dr. Marcuse told me that, confidentially, of course."

"Please, honey," his mother said, gripping his sleeve. "Don't lie like this."

"Those people at the hospital." His father waved his arm, freeing it. "They don't know who's coming or going. You know that." He stood, pushing back his chair, which moaned against the linoleum floor. His hands shook. "Where's Buddy?"

"He's asleep."

"Buddy's never asleep," his father said. "He's like Big Brother."

His father strode around the table toward the dining room. Buddy retreated, then the footsteps ceased. Heart pounding, he peeked around the corner in the dining room. His mother, half-seated, held his father's arm.

"Leave him out of this. If you don't start being straight with me, you can go."

His father glanced into the dining room, then pulled his sleeve from his mother's grip. He sidled around the table, balancing on his fingertips. When he spoke, his voice was soft and angry, like hers, yet pitched as if he knew Buddy was listening.

"You don't really mean that, Margot. You're too old to take chances. Trip's gonna want someone a lot younger, and without a child."

"This doesn't have anything to do with Trip," his mother said.

"Of course it does." His father leaned across the table. "Remember when you told me all you ever wanted was a child? I gave you one. And you said if I worked hard, to have money for that child, you'd help me any way you could? I've held up my end of that bargain, too. You think Trip would do that?"

"It wasn't like that," his mother said, reaching for his father's hands.

His father turned and faced the TV; its dead green eye reflected the yellow kitchen, and his parents somewhere inside it.

"I've been with you every step of the way," his mother said. "If this isn't good enough, I'm sorry. All I'm asking is you make a decent home for your child."

His father glanced into the dining room. This time, Buddy was sure that his father saw him. His father started toward him, past his mother's outstretched hand. Buddy scrambled to his bed, the cold floor chilling his feet. But his father was already there, stripping covers from him, his hands above him swift and calm. Shivering, Buddy curled into a tight ball.

"Leave him alone, for God's sake," his mother said. "This isn't his battle."

"He started it," his father said, in a voice that was almost joking; then, to Buddy, "Just like you started the fire? Just like you made it snow, right?"

His father bent down, so that the porch light illuminated his eyes. "What do you want?" he said. "Do you want me to stay?"

His mother tugged at his father's shoulder, starting to cry. Buddy tried to think of something, some joke that might help his father. But his father, his eyes wounded and merciless, could see his wish, and darkness covered his face when he rose.

"How dare you," his mother said, as his father pushed past her. "How dare you."

She knelt beside his bed and drew the covers up to his chin. Against his cheek, her fingers were wet and rough. "Daddy's just being silly, honey. He didn't mean anything. Go to sleep. Will you do that?"

In the doorway, his father stood with his back to them, hiding his face in his hands. His mother touched his shoulder. Buddy closed his eyes.

↗↘

When he woke, the sky had cleared, so that the night seemed infinitely blue and deep. A pockmarked moon shone down on him like a beacon. Voices rumbled from the kitchen, talking about the laboratory, but the words' bright colors were muted, as if they swam at the bottom of a dark well. Silently, Buddy rose and began to dress. He turned his two-sided jacket orange side out and went to the hallway.

In the kitchen, Trip, his mother, and his father sat at the yellow table, which was crowded with beer bottles. His mother's face was flushed and beautiful; she draped her arm across his father's shoulder. His father had removed his lab coat and loosened his tie. He stared at Trip, taking quick, nervous sips of his beer. Only Trip looked the same, and Buddy thought that it was this sameness his father coveted.

"Yeah," his father said, leaning back in his chair. "Son of a bitch threw a short. Cold can do that sometimes."

Buddy crossed a stream of light that fell from the kitchen across the dining room floor, then waited for the voices to stop. When they didn't, he groped through the dark living room and opened the front door lock, holding his breath until it clicked.

Outside, the night air gripped his face, turning it brittle with cold. Stars glinted down at him like needles. He shut the front door, taking care not to waste any heat, then covered his head with his fur-lined hood and secured the heavy brass zipper over his chin. He looked across the street for signs of the older boys, but saw none. When he stepped from the porch, the crunch of his boots made him flinch. Around him, the yards and streets were still and gray and cosseted in silence.

The snow angels were gone. The snowman's smile was blurred and sinister in the moonlight. One by one, Buddy plucked the candies from his face, but when he was done the snowman's blank stare frightened him. He turned, feeling it watch him, and set off down the row of colorless lawns. With each step, the distance to Grandma Liddy's house seemed to multiply in the streets' shadowy outlines– a miniature city, infinitely large. He remembered crossing a railroad track, and the roaring darkness beneath a pillared freeway, and his heart quailed. Until his mother called to him, he would go as far as he could, though his bootsteps whispered, though he felt himself begin to vanish.

Ariel

I met her waiting on the city bus. She was a year ahead of me at the sister school across the parking lot from my own. I can still see us: she in a khaki skirt and button-down blue shirt, myself in corduroys and dress shirt and topsiders—school uniforms, disguises. The year before, in my sophomore English class, I had read *The Odyssey;* I imagined her fair Irish face was like Pallas Athena's. I was a slouchy kid with a hard-eyed stare, the star of mimeographed literary magazines, a *poéte maudit* of high school. When I was twelve years old, five years before, my father had moved to a big house across the city from my mother and me, and I labored under the illusion that the world owed me something in return. I saw that Ariel—not her real name, the one I invented for her—was kind, and in those days, I looked for kindness everywhere. She had sharp gray eyes, a sly, teasing voice—teasing, not mocking;

23

a voice that was almost like being touched, that I can still hear today.

She asked what I was reading, and what it meant. I was reading Rimbaud—*At the age of seven, he composed fictions about life / In the vast desert, where luminous Liberty lies in her abduction.* I couldn't explain the poem to her; I didn't know what it meant. But I sat next to her on the bus, telling her about the book I was planning, a *roman à clef* about my father. Then I followed her off the bus, past identical houses with neatly manicured lawns, to her parents' house, still talking. In the neighborhood where I'd grown up, windows were caged with burglar bars; in hers were rows of modest brick suburban boxes, as mysterious to me as shrines. She closed the screen door between us, smiling, a little afraid, claiming her parents were home. I knew she was lying. But I left, exultant; I decided that I should be in love with her, and so, I was.

For months, I spent countless late-night hours on the phone, listening to her talk about her family. Sometimes her father got drunk, she said, and whipped her with a belt; her mother wouldn't stop him. Her sisters had left long ago. She had to get out of Houston, she said. Would I steal my mother's car? She knew just where to go—a fire lookout, high above the dark East Texas forest, where no one would find us.

"Would you do that for me, Turner?" she said.

I hesitated, imagining the pine forest swaying beneath us, the touch of her skin on mine, the risks of taking my mother's car, afraid I would give the wrong answer, and make a fool of myself. She laughed and said she was only kidding; I didn't believe her. Her voice was like a rope in the darkness, and I clung to it. I listened, through the crackle of static and faint conversations on other lines, to her silence, which I knew would tell me more than her words, listening for a clue, a key, that would prove whether she loved me.

Each morning, the fall I turned sixteen and my father gave me a rattletrap car for my birthday, I took Ariel to school. She teased me gently, unmercifully, tickling me, clapping her hands over my eyes as I drove. She played with me as if I were a child; and I laughed till my eyes stung with tears.

In the afternoons, having dropped her off, I slipped into a bar downtown. Since the age of twelve, I'd stolen liquor from my father's house. Now, if I wore a certain tweed jacket, my father's red silk tie, a three-day growth of beard, I could buy booze almost anywhere. In the bar, giant candles dripped, reflected in a cloudy mirror, where Otis Redding serenaded anarchist skaters, aging hippies, and me. At school, I slept through classes. Sour-stomached, in a gray fog, I made anxious resolutions; but again and again, I betrayed myself, taking the next drink.

I never told Ariel I went to the bar; I never told her about the liquor I bought on weekends. I would be redeemed, I thought, by poetry and love.

Each morning, I brought her a poem:

> *Multifoliate rose,*
> *In this broken world, abide with me;*
> *Fair love,*
> *Come live with me forever.*

On weekends, we went to the garage apartment behind my father's house. For years, when I visited my father, I had stayed in the apartment, sneaking down to the big house to thieve liquor while his girlfriend of the moment and he slept. Whole weekends, whole months, passed without our seeing each other.

I don't remember the first time Ariel and I climbed the creaking moonlit stairs that smelled of motor oil and dust, or even the first time she allowed me to undress her, with trembling hands, to exchange our virginities.

In the garage apartment, where I had built a nest for myself, crowded with castoff furniture from my father's house, we had sex, did homework, watched TV. We never went out with friends. When we made love, I insisted she look into my eyes, afraid that she would disappear into herself, slip away from me. She asked me to tie her up on the bed and tease her, foreplay she could take for hours, it seemed. When she did it to me, I quickly cried uncle, reaching for her to hold me. After she left, I felt stripped bare, alone in the apartment, pain I cured with booze, and reading—Baudelaire, Ginsberg, Verlaine—but alcohol was my medicine, my insurance.

I didn't believe her when she said she didn't understand my poems; I didn't see how different we were. At a time when code was printed in dot matrix characters on folding stacks of paper, and between our two schools, only one computer class was offered, she planned to go to a small state college to study programming. It was the future, she said—a way to escape Houston, and her parents.

My only plan that summer, before she left, was for us to stay in the apartment, maybe even spend the night together. But she always had an excuse—that she couldn't evade her family.

The last Saturday I would see her before she left, I knelt on the apartment's bare wooden floor, proffering a cheap gold ring, a rose with a minute chip of diamond in its center.

She sat on the edge of the bed, looking away from me, embarrassed, I thought, by my offering. The bedcovers, which I hadn't changed that summer, to trap her smell, were still warm from our sex. Both of us were only half-dressed; I was afraid that if I waited, she would leave.

"I can't, Turner," she said. "I'm eighteen. You're seventeen."

"Please," I said.

"I can't," she said. "I'm sorry."

"Please," I said. "Why are you doing this to me?"

"It doesn't have anything to do with you." She reached down, twisting my T-shirt in her hand, trying to pull me up, to look her in the eye. "What do you want me to do?" she said. "Stay here? That's just a dream."

I'd hoped she would go to the University of Houston; I could finish high school; the garage apartment would be our home. My head felt pierced with white-hot arrows, my face scalded with shame. I wasn't drunk; I was never drunk around her; her smell and touch and most of all the belief that I possessed her were enough. But by then, except when I was with her, I was rarely sober.

"Turner," she said, tugging at my shirt. "Look at me."

I wouldn't look at her; I wouldn't give her the satisfaction of seeing my face, when I knew she had lied every time she'd said she loved me. At the same time, all I wanted was for her to look at me, to see what she had done. "Take it," I said, holding out the ring. "Take it," I said, until she obeyed.

For a few days, I didn't see her. She wouldn't answer my calls. Late at night, alone in my mother's kitchen, I drank sweet blended whiskey, watching televangelists—Jim and Tammy Faye Baker, Pat Robertson, *The 700 Club*—until, when the weeping men embraced each other, I found myself weeping, too, before I stopped myself, embarrassed, wrung dry.

When she called to tell me she was leaving, she said she wouldn't see me. She wouldn't give me her phone number or address at the small state college she attended. It was for my own good, she said. I beat the receiver against a windowsill until my knuckles were bloody, until my mother called my father, frightened. I was acting crazy, she said, like my father had when she'd first met him. She'd known something like this would happen with Ariel. Think of that poor girl, she said. Think of what I was doing to her.

Cradling my hand against my chest, I sat on my bed, as I had when I was very young, when I had waited for my father to come home from work at the hospital. Now, as then, I listened for his car in the driveway; I listened as he and my mother bickered in the kitchen about whose mistakes could account for what I had become: my father's anger or my mother's laxity, my father's absence or my mother's coddling.

I waited, listening, as if in their words I could divine my future. Beneath my cynicism was belief, absolute belief, that they could tell me who I was.

My father peeked into my room, as he had when he'd picked me up on weekends when I was younger— awkward, abashed, a visitor in his own life. Already, I'd begun to cry, deep wracking sobs; he embraced me, as if I were still a child.

"Anything you need," he said. "It's all my fault."

A week later, I went to the psychiatrist he'd hired. In photographs from that time, I am skeletally thin. I felt like a phantom; the humid summer wind blew through me, a feeling of insouciance, of freedom from feeling.

I hated the psychiatrist, a small, pinched-looking woman who peered at me through glinting rimless glasses. My neck stiffened as I kept my gaze turned to her office window. She asked about Ariel, and I ignored her. She asked about the bandages on my knuckles, and I flinched from her, as if from a snake.

And yet, when she asked whether I drank or took drugs, I hesitated, looking out her window at the blank gray sky. I knew what would happen if I told her the truth, which I had never told anyone, not even the poets and punks with whom I drank that summer at the River Oaks Theater and the Cabaret Voltaire, many of whom had already been in recovery, all of whom, it seemed, had read *The Drama of the Gifted Child.* It would be like staging my own funeral, I thought, without the pain of actual death. It was my last best hope to bring Ariel home.

And so I told the psychiatrist about my afternoons at the bar downtown, and buying handles of whiskey from King Liquor, near my mother's house; I told her about the guitar case under my bed filled with empty bottles, and the storm drain in front of my mother's house clogged with bottles, so many the curb flooded when it rained. All of it was true, and I'd never told anyone; and as I spoke, I watched myself, unsure I could believe what I said, as if I were watching someone I didn't know.

Three weeks later, I waited for my father in the Family Room at the Avondale Recovery Clinic, a warren of cells in a strip mall in suburban Houston that smelled of carpet glue and sweat. Tinted plate-glass windows looked out at a parking lot that rippled with August heat. I sat in a chair perpendicular to two gray couches on either side of the room, which could not have been more than ten feet across. On the carpeted sound-proofed walls hung framed posters of sailboats and pre-dawn runners exhorting PERSEVERANCE and HONESTY and SUCCESS.

The next day, I would be released, against the advice of the psychiatrist and addiction counselor, to begin my last year at the all-boys' Catholic college prep a few blocks away. My time at the Clinic had passed with excruciating slowness—the heavy fact of my own body, newly reawakened, the heavy passage of time, weighted with unfulfilled desire. Worst of all were the adult AA meetings mandated by the Clinic. The alcoholics' worn, masklike faces frightened and repelled me. None of it had anything to do with me, I thought; everything at the Clinic was a sham, a grim farce. I spent my days alone in my room, writing to Ariel. I had gone to Hell, I wrote—*the sobs and insults of my own despair, / the bitter laughter of a beaten man / repeated in the sea's huge gaiety*[1]. Come back, I wrote. We can run away. We can live in the fire tower. This time, I wouldn't hesitate.

Outside, in the parking lot, my father skated across waves of shimmering heat, then barked his name into the intercom, and burst into the tiny room, wearing a sagging two-piece suit, eyeing the women fearfully. My mother, who had occupied her attention with knitting a scarf, had been asking me about the food at the Clinic, and whether I had enough clean clothes, now looked at him with distaste, and relief; it seemed to me that the psychiatrist and addiction counselor made her nervous.

The psychiatrist and the addiction counselor, a smooth-faced young woman who had been very kind to me, and whom I therefore considered rather dense, regarded him narrowly. I had made the mistake of telling her about the weekends I spent alone in the garage apartment while my father entertained his girlfriends. Now I felt guilty, as if I had betrayed him; and at the same time, pleasure in my betrayal.

It only took one look from my father to shatter that pleasure. As he sat next to my mother on the couch, he glanced at me; I could tell that all I had done had hurt

---

1. Alas, dear reader, this verse is not my own; it is from "Obsession," p. 77, *The Flowers of Evil*, by Charles Baudelaire, trans. Richard Howard, David R. Godine, Boston, 1982.

him, and I felt his injury as if it were my own.

I'd made significant progress, the addiction counselor said, nodding, her Mickey Mouse earrings swinging in unison as she spoke; I participated in group and individual therapy, shared appropriately at AA meetings, even created beautiful stained-glass pieces in art therapy.

"But this is just a start," she said. "We need to keep hitting our meetings, going to therapy, working the program."

She glanced at the psychiatrist, a cue.

"We are concerned," the psychiatrist said. "We know you've spent a lot of your time here writing to Ariel. We think you have formed an unhealthy attachment to her. Do you know what a fetish is?"

"Yes," I said. *It's my dick*, I thought.

"A fetish is an object we think has power. But it doesn't, until we give it power. Its power depends upon us, not it."

I looked out at the cars shimmering in the heat, imagining stealing one of them, fleeing to Ariel. I knew what the psychiatrist meant—that Ariel herself didn't matter. The psychiatrist knew nothing about love and poetry. My skin felt flayed and my nerves cried out for a cigarette; if this was what being sober meant, I thought, I didn't want it.

"You need to focus," the addiction counselor said. "It's easy to get lost in other people. It's time to look at yourself. We don't think it's a healthy choice for you to contact Ariel. We've talked to your mother about this, and she agrees."

My mother glanced up from her knitting; I smirked at

her, as we always had when I'd gotten in trouble, as if what was happening was a joke. But she met my gaze squarely, and I saw what I had not seen, until that moment—that she wasn't nervous, but afraid.

"Let me make it simple," the addiction counselor said. "You need to decide what you really love—yourself, or Ariel, or the booze."

I rolled my eyes, to hide my panic.

My father raised his hand.

"I know I should have been around more for Turner," he said, staring down at his hands, which were clenched, as if in prayer. "I should have kept a better eye on him these last few years. I should have listened when he said he wanted to go to the high school for the performing arts. I know what that's like. When I was Turner's age, I wanted to be a painter, but my mother wouldn't let me. She wanted me to be a doctor."

The addiction counselor started to speak, but my father lifted his hand again, to silence her; he leaned forward on the couch, elbows on his knees, his sadness filling the room. "What I'm trying to say," he said, "is everyone has just a few chances at a happy life. So I think Turner should see his girl, if that's what's going to make him happy."

He was like Elvis, I thought, like Reagan, irresistible. His words were like a drug. I knew I shouldn't believe him, but I did.

"Thank you," the addiction counselor said. "We will take that into consideration in our treatment plan."

"I'm just saying," my father said. "I wish I'd done more to make him happy."

"You," the addiction counselor said to my father. "You want to make yourself happy." Then, to me, the rictus of her smile gone: "It's your life. A matter of life and death."

The point was moot. That fall, Ariel didn't call or write. For a while, I tried to get her address from her friends, but they wouldn't help me. My mother told me that if I went to find Ariel at her college, she, my mother, would have me arrested.

And then, other things happened. I went back to school, where I found I enjoyed my newfound lucidity. Each Friday night, I attended the adult AA meeting at the Clinic, and though the alcoholics' masklike faces still frightened me, and I shunned their attempts to befriend me, I felt safe, as if in their faces I could see my future, whether to court, or avoid. One of the men, Jim G., who wore black Brylcreemed hair and a ravaged salesman's face, repeated the same story each meeting—three wives, two jobs, one son, all lost to booze. At first, I thought his story merely glib, but I came to understand that he repeated it like a rosary, to remind him of what he had lost, not so that he could bring it back, but so that he could learn to live with his losses.

Ariel receded from me. I had believed—not long before—that this would mean I myself would cease to exist. When it didn't, I felt as if I had woken from a long, dark dream into daylight. I remembered the letters I'd written to her at the Clinic, and cringed at their calculation and insincerity. I put away the Ginsberg and Verlaine; I picked up T. S. Eliot and Teilhard de Chardin. I stayed sober, because I was afraid of what would happen to me if I didn't.

A few days before Christmas, the phone rang at my mother's house. The instant I put the heavy receiver to my ear and heard the staticky silence, I knew it was Ariel; and in an instant, all the months since I had seen her vanished.

"Turner," she said. "Are you okay?"

I don't remember what I answered. I felt the room go dark, blotted out by my own desire; and I was unused to answering this question honestly.

"I need to see you," she said.

I don't remember what I said, or how we made a plan to meet at the garage apartment; I only remember the fierce quicksilver pull of lust, and looking at the cuneiform marks on the windowsill where I had struck it with the phone I now held, and the fear and expectation of what would happen when I saw her again.

A few days later, I left my mother's house wearing the tweed jacket, my father's red silk tie, three days' growth of beard, lifting twenty dollars from her purse. I told her I was going out with friends; she knew that I was lying.

Don't do it, Turner, she said. Don't be a fool.

I drove, flicking ash out the side vent window of the rattletrap car into a stream of frigid wind, past the machine shops and vacant fields near my mother's house, past the El Destino Lounge #2, where men gathered outside its doorway, a block of light and darkness beneath a sky glowing gold and purple.

I checked the dashboard clock—half-past six—King Liquor would stay open until nine. I wanted what I always wanted—the first light buzz, the first sprinkling of fairy dust that would transform the bottomless longing I'd felt, even before Ariel's call—the longing when I saw the Christmas billboards in Spanish ("*Budweiser hace un vero Feliz Navidad*"), or the pinkish light of the Christmas tree in my mother's living room, which my father used to put up—into something merely wistful. It never worked; inevitably, I chased that feeling into oblivion.

I drove, over the railroad tracks, to the freeway. I told myself the jacket and tie and three-day beard were only insurance, that I wouldn't take a drink that night.

I sat in the rattletrap car outside my father's house on a street near Rice University overspread with lost maples and live oaks, smoking, trying to calm myself, shivering in the thin tweed jacket. Shadows moved like ghosts through the trees. My chest felt stuffed with cotton; I told myself I should leave, but I couldn't.

Past the big house, a window in the garage apartment was faintly lit. The windows of the big house were dark, the house itself bare of the Christmas lights that outlined other houses on the street, though on the front lawn were the glowing plastic Santa and reindeer my father placed dutifully each year on his lawn. I got out of the car, fearing, as I always did when I walked through the yard, that one of his neighbors would call the police. I tried to feel contempt for the decorations, for the two-story mock-Tudor house which stretched across two lots—shallow, cramped, an empty façade, I thought—trying to resist the sadness I felt, looking at it; I remembered when my father had bought it five years before, when he still haunted my mother's house, spending nights with her on weekends. That summer, he and I worked together in the big house, climbing into the attic to wire burglar alarms, pulling up carpet and picking tacks out of the floor. I had been happy. My father never hinted that he would bring my mother and me there to live with him; I'd been happy because I believed he would, in the stubborn, hermetic way children believe what they wish to be true.

I knocked on the garage apartment door, then opened it. Ariel had used a spare key under the doormat. The ceiling light was on in the bedroom, which except for a short hallway, bathroom, and closet was the whole of the apartment. I'd spent my weekends there much as I had before, chain-smoking, reading, trying to write my own poems, alone. The dusty, oily-smelling air grew warmer as I ascended the stairs, my heart thudding, imagining what I would find in the bedroom—Ariel sitting in a chair, arms crossed, glowering at me; or beckoning me, naked in bed.

Ariel—or the person I had called Ariel, because it was clear to me in an instant, from the baggy college sweatshirt she wore, from her hair cropped as short as my own, that she was no longer the person I had known, though none of these changes could account for the change I saw in her—sat at the brown wood laminate table in the middle of the room, reading a book, peering at it furiously with her sharp gray eyes, as if she could penetrate its meaning with her gaze alone. I knew she'd heard me. Her feigned ignorance was a familiar trick, which had intimidated me; now, I understood that it was shyness.

"I don't get it," she said, tossing the book closed, so that it slid across the table. I saw it was Rimbaud; I saw that she wore the gold rose ring.

My heart leapt. She looked at me, then, in a way that unsettled me, as if she were afraid. I could not imagine why she would be afraid of me. She had all the power, I thought—the power to make me feel leaden with despair, or my heart soar with hope.

"You're all dressed up," she said. "Are you going out?"

I hesitated, believing for a moment she could see the meaning of the jacket and tie; but of course, she couldn't see this, I thought.

"Sure," I said.

Her grey eyes shifted uncertainly; and I found I enjoyed my fleeting power.

"Tell me what it's about," she said, tapping the book. "Pick one."

I hadn't read Rimbaud since I'd been to the Clinic; I was afraid of what it might do to me if I touched it. Now I opened it at random:

> *Sweeter than children find the taste of sour fruit,*
> *Green water filled my cockle shell of pine.*
> *Anchor and rudder went drifting away,*
> *Washed in vomit and stained with blue wine.*
>
> *Now I drift through the Poem of the Sea;*
> *This gruel of stars mirrors the milky sky,*
> *Devours green azures; ecstatic flotsam,*
> *Drowned men, pale and thoughtful, sometimes drift by.*

I knew what the poem meant—at least, more than before I'd gone to the Clinic; it meant what I saw in the adult alcoholics' masklike faces, and heard in Jim G.'s story of his three wives, two jobs, one son. But I couldn't explain any of this to Ariel; I didn't want to explain it. I shrugged and lay the book on the table.

"Are you okay?" she said.

She watched me—it wasn't fear I saw, but something else. I sat at the table and reached for her hand, hoping to deflect her question. She moved her hand away, covering it with her other hand.

"Why didn't you tell me?" she said. "You lied to me. I could have helped."

I saw, now, that she wasn't afraid; she was angry.

"I didn't tell anyone," I said.

"But I'm not anyone," she said, glaring at me.

Her eyes were pinkish, glassy with tears; I reached for her hands, but she moved them from me again. "I was so mad at you," she said. "I called your mother and she said it was true, you were in that place, and then I called that place and they wouldn't let me see you."

I thought of my mother glancing up from her crocheting at the Clinic. She had known all along. Rage flashed through me, a warmth like a shot of whiskey.

"You talked to my mother?"

"She told me what happened to you. She told me you were drinking so much they had to put you into that place. That you almost died."

What she said was true. The addiction counselor said if I kept drinking as I had, I would not survive. At the time, I'd dismissed it; even then, sitting across from Ariel, I didn't know if it was true. Ariel covered her face with her hands. Her shoulders shook and crying sounds came from behind her hands. I had never imagined she would cry for me. A warm choking feeling closed in my throat. I touched her shoulder, but she shrank from me.

"I'm sorry," I said.

She turned from me; I lay my hand on her shoulder, feeling the humid warmth of her skin.

"I'm sorry," I said.

"I hate it up there, Turner. I'm flunking English. I don't have any friends. I think I'm going to transfer," she said, uncovering her face; and in her eyes, I saw, now, behind her diffidence and anger, what I had not seen before—a fickle girl, a foolish girl, someone foolish enough to mistake her own sadness for love.

"Will you stay here for me, Turner?"

I remembered her asking me to steal my mother's car and take her to the fire tower, how I had waited, listening, to see if she would make a fool of me.

"Yes," I said, taking her hand.

"Turner," she said. "Why'd you do it? Why'd you go there?"

I felt the rough edges of the rose ring, the warmth of her breath on my face. I remembered staring out the window of the psychiatrist's office, watching myself, not knowing whether to believe what I said. I knew, then, sitting with Ariel, that I had told the psychiatrist the truth; but I also knew that I would never tell the truth to Ariel.

Now, many years later, standing at a window in a locked detox ward in Brookline, Massachusetts, I remember this moment, watching a line of school children holding hands, their figures dark against a field of snow. My hands, on the window, tremble like spiders walking across water. I am here, in the ward, after another failed romance, though I know that romance has nothing to do with why I am here.

"For you," I said to Ariel, then.

Her grey eyes hardened, unsure whether to believe me. Then she looked at me as I had wanted her to for a long time, trusting me, surrendering to me; but I felt no pleasure, only a sickening thrum of sadness, and contempt.

"It's true," I said, leaning closer to her. "I went there for you."

The trees above my father's house swam in the dark night wind. Ariel—or the person I had called Ariel—had told me she could spend the night; she was in college now. I told her I needed to get cigarettes—a cliché, of which I was ashamed, even then. In the dark apartment, everything had been as I imagined, or remembered, it—the smell of detergent on her clothes, the taste of her mouth, the slight roughness of her skin. While we made love, she had kept her eyes locked on mine. And yet, when I lay holding her, instead of longing to stay with her there forever, all I wanted was to flee. I sat in my car, lit a cigarette, my hands trembling, and opened the tiny side window to vent the smoke, already ghostly, feeling the lightness of the twenty dollars in my pocket. The dashboard clock read half past eight. I told myself I'd done the right thing, though I couldn't think of what I'd done. Love and poetry were for suckers, I thought. I glanced up at the dark windows in my father's house, and felt the old, deep longing, the old, deep wounds, and knew I would always be my father's son. I started the car and set off, down the tree-tunneled street, toward the freeway and my mother's house, delaying from moment to moment what I knew would come— what I welcomed, what I feared, coming toward me in the darkness.

King Elvis

When Buddy was eight years old, he wanted to see Elvis Presley *Live! In Concert* at the Hofheinz Pavilion. The show was a month away, but the ad in the Houston Post warned that tickets would soon be sold out. When Buddy told his mother about the concert, and the price of the tickets, she said they would have to ask his father.

"What's he got to do with it?" Buddy said.

His mother gave him a look. "He's your father."

"So?"

"So we'll have to ask him first."

For almost a year, while his father had been away, Buddy had impersonated the King, donning a white vest trimmed with gold brocade and colored beads, gyrating his hips on the front porch for the neighbor girls, Cara and Darlene Knight. Some of the older neighbors, retirees from Hughes Tool, up the street, complained about what they called his caterwauling. Buddy wanted to remind them that the King Himself had begun his career singing on street corners in Tupelo, Mississippi; but his mother said that sometimes people didn't care to be persuaded.

His mother had made the vest for his birthday. She'd also made him lion tamer and mad scientist and magician outfits. When he was very young, and his father was still in medical school in Galveston, she had made him a cassock he wore around the neighborhood in imitation of St. Patrick, and St. Francis of Assisi, whose stories she had read to him from *The Lives of the Saints*. One day, when he was using a shamrock to explain to his mother the mystery of the Holy Trinity, he realized that he did not believe what he was saying, and worse, that he did not believe in God. The thought struck him mute with shame and terror, and he never revealed it.

His mother was very religious. In a window above the kitchen sink, where she often stood and watched the sunset, was a stained glass window-hanging of the Holy Family, their faces blank haloed ovals; a picture of a church that said "Go to Him, visit with Him, pray to Him;" a small plastic Jesus who had somehow been beheaded.

Each weekday she picked up Buddy in their dusty green car, wearing her white hospital uniform, smelling of laboratory chemicals. Sometimes they stopped at the grocery store, or at McDonald's for a treat. Weekends, they took stacks of newspapers to Queen of Peace for the church paper drive, and on Sundays, they bought barbecue after Mass. Because she had faith, she said, his mother met most events calmly. Her favorite saying was to let go and let God. Only when her father called did her face, usually placid, and her eyes, curious and sometimes sharp, become worried. The phone rang, and the air in the house became heavy and still.

His father had gone to Detroit to finish medical school. Soon, he would have to enter the Army to serve out his draft deferment. He had chosen to go to Detroit, his mother said, because it was a better residency than Galveston; but with the Army, she said, his father had no choice. For months before his father moved to Detroit, she and his father had talked in their room at night. Their voices sounded like they belonged to people he didn't know: his mother's thin and pleading, his father's flat and deep, a shutting door. Now it would be another year until his father returned.

After his father left for Detroit, Buddy watched Elvis' last comeback concert, *Elvis: Aloha from Hawaii,* on TV. The Elvis then didn't look like the Elvis his father had pointed out to him in Saturday afternoon movies, who curled his lip and swung his guitar while women screamed. The new Elvis gazed distantly at the audience, his movements slow and sad, as if he did not quite know where he was. Women did not scream. Heads bowed, they approached the stage, and Elvis, kneeling, hung garlands of flowers around their necks, as if he were a kind of priest.

And yet, Elvis was still the King. Buddy's father said so when he'd called, and Buddy told him what he thought of the concert.

"He's a fake," Buddy said. "He's been retired too long."

"What would the King say about that?" His father's voice sank, grew wooly and deep. "Hold on." His father put his hand over the receiver. A muffled conversation ensued. "This-a Evvis," his father said, in the new voice. "I hear you been callin' me a fake. I'm a-gonna sic the

Memphis Mafia on you."

"You do that," Buddy said. "You aren't tough enough to do it yourself."

"Uh-huh-huh," said Elvis. "I'm comin' back."

"I don't believe you," Buddy said.

Twice, Buddy had visited his father in Detroit. The first time was at Christmas, not long after he'd seen the comeback concert. On the plane, his mother gripped Buddy's hand and told him not to worry, that God would provide. He hadn't worried, until she'd said that. When they got to Detroit, as they drove toward downtown, near Henry Ford Hospital, where he lived, his father cursed the snow and the traffic. He seemed to be in a great hurry, though why this was so, Buddy couldn't tell.

Over the next few days, Buddy's mother took pictures of him standing outside his father's crumbling brownstone, and of Buddy and his father opening gifts at his kitchen table, and of Buddy's father showing him specimens in the lab where he worked. Later, Buddy remembered, though he could not find them in the pictures, jars of stillborn babies, like Jesse Garon, Elvis' stillborn twin. His father's apartment smelled of roach spray and sweat, and he had put a sickly green electric sign in his window that said ROOMS. His father lived, Buddy thought, in Heartbreak Hotel.

Buddy listened to his mother's and father's voices seep from his father's room, as the sign cast its long green shadows across the ceiling, and pipes pinged and sighed.

I'll wait for you, his mother said. But I can't just leave.

There's the house, my job, his friends. Our whole life.

If you loved me, his father said, none of that would matter.

It's not that simple.

That was one goddamned nurse. That was a long time ago.

I want to trust you. But I need to be sure.

This is why I left, his father said. Because you don't believe in me.

In the spring, Buddy went to Detroit by himself. Because he was a big boy, his mother said. Buddy didn't believe her. Between Christmas and then, his mother had cried each time she'd talked on the phone to his father. She cried when she took Buddy to the airport, too, and told him that God would take care of him. On the plane, Buddy imagined that he was a spy on a mission so secret that he did not know what it was.

In Detroit, his father walked stiffly, as if pulled by invisible strings. He said that he needed to use the phone, and spoke in a voice so quiet that Buddy couldn't understand his words. They visited places, though his father didn't seem to care where they went: The Ford Motor Museum, the fairgrounds at Grosse Ile, the Indian Theater. Buddy missed buying barbecue after Mass, and bundling newspapers for the church drive, and even the crying room he'd once thought was Purgatory, and Father Peron's droning homilies.

The last day he was there, Buddy and his father visited the laboratory where Thomas Edison had invented the light bulb and phonograph. Henry Ford had moved the building from Dearborn, Michigan, plank by plank. After the tour, they sat on an iron bench and kept their hands in the pockets of their jackets. In the park, trees with bare branches hunched like skeletons. His father was very quiet.

"How do you like living with your mother?" his father asked.

His breath made scraps of steam in the gray air. Steam was made, they had learned that day, by the condensation of water.

"Fine," Buddy said.

"You think you might like living here?" his father said.

The planks of lumber of Thomas Edison's laboratory had been numbered and carried on horse-drawn carts built specially for that purpose.

"I don't know," Buddy said.

"Think about it," his father said.

"Yes, sir."

"When I get to wherever the Army is going to send me, maybe you can live with me there," his father said, more loudly. "How'd you like that?"

A bright yellow leaf was stuck on the black asphalt path. Buddy didn't answer.

His father shook his head. "With my luck, they'll send me to some shithole, just like they did Elvis. Fort Hood. Jesus H. Christ. He was never the same.

"Buddy?" his father said.

His father's face was frightened. "Things are going to change, Buddy," he said. "I might not live at your house when I get back. You're going to need to decide where you want to live. Understand?"

The yellow leaf didn't move; the yellow leaf was a fact.

The Thursday after he found the ad for the concert, Buddy stood between his mother and the phone in the kitchen. They were waiting for his father to call, as he did at the same time each week. Buddy had already hinted to Cara and Darlene and some boys at school that he was going to see Elvis, though he hadn't mentioned this to his mother. They should have bought tickets the day he'd seen the ad, he said; they might already be gone. His mother pointed out that, aside from the tickets' outrageous price, the concert was on a school night. If his father lived with them, she said, he would definitely have something to say about that. But he didn't live with them, Buddy said, so why should he have anything to say about anything?

"That's irrelevant," his mother said.

"I think it is," Buddy said, unsure what she meant.

The phone rang.

"Move it or lose it," his mother said, reaching for the phone.

"Honey?" she said in a different voice. "Is that you? Hold on a second." She cupped her hand over the receiver, her eyes already clouded.

"You can talk to daddy later," she said.

He went to the corner in the hallway where noise bounced back from the kitchen; he always listened there to his mother talk with his father on the phone. His mother asked his father, as usual, how much call his father was taking, if his apartment was warm—Buddy waited impatiently for her to mention the concert.

"He's got some idea about an Elvis concert," she said. "You know I don't like that kind of music, honey, but he's just crazy to go. I think he wants to go with you. I know you can't. I'm not trying to play games with you. I'm not trying to turn him against you. Every day, he gets angrier and sadder and further away from God—I'm telling you about your son. I know it was my decision, but we can't do anything about that now. I need to know what you're going to do when you come back."

Buddy went to his room. He had heard enough. They were not going to talk about the concert, and the tickets would be sold out. His mother kept asking his father the same question. And his father kept asking him where he wanted to live when he came back from the Army. Months ago, when he'd returned from Detroit, Buddy could have told his mother what his father had asked him, but he hadn't. He kept waiting for something to happen, but he didn't even know what.

The walls of his room were yellow. In his closet were an Army surplus helmet and gas mask his father had sent him. On a low table near a window were the bottles and vials of his laboratory. Above his bed, his mother's picture of the Virgin of Guadalupe regarded him mildly. Leaning against a wall was a thin mattress from a child's single bed, its blue, shiny material worn at the center in a dull, stained oval.

He grabbed an imaginary microphone, clutched the neck of an imaginary guitar. He imagined a giant dark hall of screaming fans. He curled his lip; the crowd went wild. He snapped his fingers, ground its toe into the floor as if he were grinding out a bug, hips swiveling, swinging his

arm, like a sheet snapping in the wind. *You ain't nothin'
but a hound dog, cryin' all the time*, he sang, to the Virgin.
You know you ain't nothin' and you ain't no friend of mine.
He spun into the mattress, bounced off it, crouched in
a karate stance. *You said you were high class, well that was
just a lie. You know you ain't nothing and you ain't no friend
of mine.* He lunged at the mattress, beat it with his hand.
He beat it until his hand stung, until his mother called
him to the phone.

Until Buddy talked to his father, his mother said, next
Thursday, she wouldn't buy the tickets. She said Buddy
had hurt his father's feelings by not coming to the phone
the Thursday before. By then, it was only two Saturdays
before the concert. Buddy wasn't even sure he wanted to
see Elvis anymore; he remembered the slow, sad Elvis he'd
seen in the comeback concert. Some of the boys at school
had called Elvis a redneck. But even if he didn't want to see
Elvis, his mother said, he still owed his father an apology.

"We're still a family," she said. "We have to act like
one."

She tried phoning his father that afternoon, then again
later that night, then several times on Sunday. "I'm sorry
to bother you, honey," she said, when she finally reached
him. "Did they keep you on call?"

His father's voice crackled through the receiver, loud
enough for Buddy to hear, though not to understand what
he said. His mother flinched. "Buddy has something he
wants to say to you," she said.

She held out the receiver, then went to the kitchen sink. She stood at the window with the Holy Family and the beheaded Jesus and the picture of the church. On the phone, his father's voice was flat and harsh.

"What's on your mind?" his father said.

"I'm sorry," Buddy said.

"What are you sorry for?"

"I'm sorry I didn't talk to you."

His father made a dismissive noise. "You still want to see Elvis?"

"I think so."

"Tell your mother to get the tickets. Tell her I'll pay for them."

"Thank you," Buddy said.

"Have you thought any more about what we talked about?"

"No," Buddy said.

"You need to think about it. Is your mother listening?"

"I think so."

"Tell her to leave. Tell her I want to talk to you alone."

"I can't."

"Why not?" his father said. "I'm getting tired of this bullshit."

"I'm sorry, dad," Buddy said. "Thank you for the tickets."

Buddy and his mother hurried across the parking lot to Hofheinz Pavilion. Buddy wore his white vest. Cara and Darlene had told him to try to remember every song, so he could do the concert for them afterward. Even the boys at school had seemed impressed that he was going out on a school night. When they'd gone to the box office two weeks ago, his mother had crouched in front of him and asked if he was sure he wanted to do this. He was sure, he'd said. And then he'd felt something cold and terrible, like when he'd known he didn't believe in God.

At the Hofheinz Pavilion, men in fluorescent orange vests told them to hurry; it was almost time for the show. His mother had warned Buddy that he would make a spectacle out of himself in his vest. But in the glass-walled rotunda outside the arena, among the swarm of people, many of whom looked old enough to be their retired neighbors, many were dressed like Elvis: early Elvises in pink silk shirts, checkered coats, and blue suede shoes; late Elvises in white jumpsuits and mirrored sunglasses; one late Elvis flashed Buddy the secret TCB hand signal, and Buddy wondered if he'd just glimpsed the King incognito. Booths sold Elvis T-shirts, hats, silk jackets, lamps, lunch boxes, wall hangings, coffee mugs, commemorative plaques, alarm clocks and wall clocks, records, even life-sized inflatable replicas of The King. A painting of a weeping Elvis made Buddy stop; it reminded him of his mother's picture of the Blessed Virgin, and of something he couldn't name.

"Come on," his mother said, tugging his arm.

They found their seats at the lip of the arena, which smelled of popcorn and tennis shoes from the basketball games that were usually played there. Beneath them, tiny people milled, their voices indistinguishable, like at church. At one end of the arena, facing the floor seats, was a giant black curtain. His mother took a crochet hook out of her purse and began to work on a scarf for his father. After she had picked Buddy up from school, she'd dropped him off at home, because she'd had to go back to the hospital to finish work; then she'd changed her clothes and taken a shower, and they'd had just enough time to go to McDonald's before the show.

"We're too far away," Buddy said. "We can't see anything."

"We can see just fine," his mother said.

"I bet all those people down there didn't have to ask anybody if they could go. I bet they didn't have to waste a bunch of time waiting to talk to somebody."

"You should be grateful you're here at all," his mother said, as she pearled.

A giddy ache tickled his throat. "I bet all those people down there don't have to say they're grateful. I bet they don't kowtow to some big fake."

His mother laid the scarf in her lap and glared at him. "If you're not satisfied, then we can leave. I mean it. I've had about enough."

He turned and looked down at the people—all of the different people, Elvis and non-Elvis; they were facts, like the leaf, not-him. "I don't see why we have to ask him for everything. I don't see why we have to do what he says."

"He is your father. We can't just run away."

"What if he doesn't come back?" He couldn't resist; it was like touching a cut. "Maybe he won't come back. Maybe I'll just go live with him."

His mother didn't answer him.

The lights fell. A gentle roar arose from the audience,

like the sound of an ocean. His mother, next to him, vanished, and for a moment, he regretted what he'd said. But this was only a childish thought. He sat on the edge of his seat, watching the stage. A band played fast music, then a spotlight illuminated a man in a loud checkered coat, not-Elvis. For a moment, Buddy felt cheated, then panicked, wondering if somehow they had gone to the wrong concert. The man told jokes Buddy didn't understand, but which he could tell, from his mother's tightened mouth, were dirty. Then the man was gone, and a line of Black men in turquoise sequined jumpsuits danced in a line to jumpy music, like fish at the bottom of a deep lake.

Then the curtain swept closed on the turquoise men and the hall went dark.

Kettledrums thundered. Trumpets blared. The crowd let out a gasp, as if until that moment, they had held their breaths. Now, Buddy sat on the edge of his seat, awake. A tiny figure in a white sequined jumpsuit prowled the stage. The crowd roared. It was unmistakable that he was Elvis. It was unmistakable that he was the King. He struck a karate pose. *I'm just a hunk-a hunk-a burnin' love*, he sang, the bellbottoms of his white jumpsuit flaring, the rings on his fingers glittering. The crowd went wild, just as Buddy had imagined—and for a moment, he imagined the crowd was cheering for him.

Elvis fell to his knees, swept out his hand, commanding the orchestra to stop, holding his microphone with the tips of his bejeweled fingers; he bowed, panting deeply. The songs became slower, unknown to Buddy; the ones he did know were like furniture in his aunt's living room.

He remembered what his father said about Elvis after he'd left the Army—that he had never been the same. He dozed again, until he was woken by the drone of an organ.

Deep blue light bathed the stage. Yellow flames twinkled in the darkness. Even his mother leaned forward in her seat. Buddy felt as if he were waking out of a dream into another dream. Elvis knelt, his cape outspread on the stage, and in the darkness, his voice boomed, tremulous, commanding:

Amazing Grace, how sweet the sound
That saved a wretch like me
I once was lost, but now am found
T'was blind but now I see.

Before the stage, a line of women had formed. Even from far away, Buddy could see their upturned, supplicant faces, shining in the blue light. As he sang the ancient hymn, Elvis placed white scarves around his neck, then around the necks of the women, who bowed their heads to receive them.

Buddy stood, pulled at his mother's hand, trying to pull her into the aisle. She shushed him, told him to stop. But it was too important to stop, too important to explain. He wanted his mother to go, to receive the blessing of the King. He kept pulling at his mother's immoveable weight.

No One's Trash

Outside the kitchen, past the glassed-in storm door, rain lashed the back yard, which was already filling up with water. On the TV, light poles littered the streets, and freeway underpasses were ponds where windshields peeked out like frogs. Margot hoped Jimmy wouldn't be foolish enough to drive across Houston to pick up Buddy; though she didn't want to begrudge Jimmy their time together, either.

The boy sat in front of the TV, his back to her, rigid as a mannequin, the usual mood he assumed when Jimmy came to get him on Saturdays. Margot had left the back door open to keep an eye on the pecan tree that swayed over the fence with Mr. Knight's back yard. What good it would do to watch it fall on her garage, she didn't know. Even through the thrum of rain and air conditioner's moan and the TV announcers' gabble, she could hear the

Knights arguing next door.

Just as she told Buddy to say a prayer that his father would be safe, the lights in the house went out, the TV went dead, the air conditioner stopped. The boy glanced back at her—she was standing at the sink, checking the road, which was still clear—then he leaned across the piles of paper on her desk, pressing his nose against the air conditioner to catch the last cool drops, his eyes closed, beatific, as if receiving a sacrament. How delicate he still was, she thought, his milk-pale skin covering blue veins, his wrists so small she could circle them with her forefinger and thumb. All morning, he hadn't spoken to her; she still wasn't sure if he would now. Her heart constricted with tenderness for him, a physical ache.

Outside, there was only the steady thrum of rain. Even the Knights had fallen silent. Margot wanted to say something, but felt suddenly shy. It was a foolish thing, a humiliating thing, she thought, to feel this way with one's own son.

The phone rang. She nearly jumped out of her skin; in the sudden quiet, it was uncanny and absurd. Buddy looked at her, then the phone, an accusation.

It could only be one of two people: Jimmy, or her mother. It was Jimmy. All morning, Margot had called the lab, and Jimmy's beeper, and his parents' house, where Jimmy said he lived. Jimmy's mother answered, and asked Margot who she thought she was, calling her son at all hours, hounding him, before she hung up. Jimmy's voice, now, was falsely causal, as if he'd just gone to the grocery store and was phoning to see if there was anything he could bring back. He asked how they were doing, in a tone that suggested he still lived with them, a tone that never failed to jolt her with anger at its presumption, and relief that it was no longer true. She said they were fine. He asked her about the backyard. She said that it was fine, too, that it hadn't taken on any water, and thanked him for putting in the drain, which was what she knew he wanted to hear. The boy glared at her, catching her lie; she turned her back on him.

"I'm not going to be able to make it over there today," Jimmy said.

"Of course not," she said, too quickly.

"Have you thought anymore about the letter?" he said.

It was all she thought about. "Not yet," she said.

Buddy watched her. He'd understood, she saw, that Jimmy wouldn't come, his expression clearing—relief, and also anger.

"I'm sorry," Jimmy said. "Tell him I'm sorry."

"Tell him yourself," she said.

The boy cradled the receiver against his shoulder, turning from her, giving mumbled one-word answers to the questions Jimmy always asked: How was school that week? How was his horror movie coming along? He told Jimmy he loved him, too, then put the receiver back in its cradle. Then he jumped up and down silently, shaking his fists, baring gritted teeth—a hateful, sorrowing dance. She had borne this kind of anger before from Jimmy. Now she couldn't look at him, at Buddy, her own son.

Outside, she saw the Knight girls, Cara and Darla, hop across the paving stones in the back yard, like naiads, like water sprites, already soaked to the bone.

"Get rid of them," Buddy said, his mouth pinched

and vindictive.

"I can't do that," she said.

She couldn't, even if she had wanted to; they were already at her door.

When she'd bought the house, right after Buddy was born, Mr. Knight's house had been a tiny, sloped-roof, two-bedroom bungalow. Since then, Mr. Knight had added a corrugated aluminum carport, and a pink, boxlike, asbestos-shingled second story that looked as if a mobile home had landed on its roof; he'd walled in the front porch, hung heavy drapes on the windows, sealing up the house against the outside world.

She laid towels on the kitchen floor, scolding the girls for their thoughtlessness in not even using an umbrella, while they dripped and stared down at their bare dirty feet; they were used to being scolded. Both of them wore the same cheap pink polyester shorts they'd worn all summer, and matching T-shirts with two tie-dye hand prints below the message: HANDS OFF. Margot wondered if their mother had bought the T-shirts for them. Her son stared at Cara with a vacant, fixed expression. Darla watched him with puppy dog eyes. Cara pretended not to notice his stare, though she kept her arms crossed tightly over her chest. When it was just Darla and Buddy, they got along fine, but when Cara was there, it was almost always a disaster.

Cara was as tall and gangly as a colt, with a long, pretty face men would find attractive. She was already going on dates, though she was barely fifteen. Margot thought that she had escaped the brunt of Mr. Knight's violence. Darla, three years younger, her son's age, was by far the more intelligent of the two, and would be more beautiful, neither necessarily an advantage. In the past year, she had gained weight, become spooky and withdrawn.

"What were you thinking," Margot said, using a tone, getting the girls in line, "coming over here, dripping all over my floor?"

"Yes, ma'am," Cara said. "We're sorry. We didn't have time."

"What do you mean, you didn't have time?"

Cara glanced at her, hesitating, caught.

"Do your parents know you're over here?" Margot demanded.

"No, ma'am," Cara said. "The lights went out and we ran."

"They're crazy, ma'am," Darla said. "They been fighting all day. Mamma yelling at Daddy to leave us alone. They're both crazy."

"Hush, Darla," Cara said, quietly.

Neither of the girls would look at her. Now she would have to call the Knights, too, after she got them settled. She couldn't send them back home. Maybe she would just let Mrs. Knight find them. But that would only make matters worse.

"Okay," she said. "I'll get you some dry clothes. Then I'm going to call your mother. You put me in a tight spot."

They grinned. They had gotten what they wanted, she thought; they wouldn't have to go back home.

"Thank you, ma'am," they said, bright as bells.

Margot shooed Buddy out of the kitchen, through the dining room, into her bedroom. She rummaged in her closet for dresses. Without the ceiling light, her closet was dark as a tomb. Nothing of Buddy's would fit them, except maybe his underwear. She went to the big open closet in his room, where she could see better, and pulled out shirts and pants of Jimmy's that still hung there. They would be too big in the waist for Cara and too long for them both, but somehow, they might work.

"What are you doing?" her son said.

"What does it look like I'm doing? I'm giving them something to wear."

"You're crazy," he said. "You've gone crazy."

She slid the hangers across the metal pole with a satisfying scritch, pulling out Jimmy's blue jeans and short-sleeved dress shirts.

"Why can't we tell them to leave? Grandmother says they're trash."

"Hush," she said. "Lower your voice."

Grandmother was Jimmy's mother, Arlene. Margot knew Arlene's opinion of her and of the neighborhood where she lived.

"Do you believe everything Grandmother says?"

"No," he said, lowering his eyes.

"No one's trash," she said. "Maybe people called Grandma Liddy and my father that when we didn't have money. Maybe people called Grandmother that when she didn't. But it doesn't mean anything. Understand?"

"Yes," he said.

"Stay here," she said. "I'm going to help them change. And then you're going to play nice with them. Understand?"

Estelle Knight answered on the first ring. Margot asked her if their power was out, and Estelle said that it was; then she told Estelle that she had the girls there, bracing herself for what would come next. Estelle was a difficult woman, whom years of marriage to Donald Knight had not improved. She had a sharp face and a beady gamine stare. Margot thought, in her less charitable moments, that Estelle was just intelligent enough to be vicious. She had railed against Margot in the past, accusing her of trying to steal the girls, a charge so absurd Margot recognized it as a sign of her desperation.

Today was more of the same. Of course, Margot had her children—*chirren*, Estelle said, Margot couldn't help but note. That's where they always were, Estelle said. Margot Liddy, she said, holier-than-thou, with her churchgoing and her fancy degree, who couldn't keep a man in her house, who had to send her son away every weekend with his father. Maybe that's why Margot was always tempting her girls over there. Maybe Margot needed to get her own house in order.

Margot looked through the storm door at the pecan tree, at the water in the yard lapping toward the garage door, upbraiding herself for the tears that pricked her eyes. Estelle's viciousness, she knew, was a consequence of her suffering.

"Estelle," she said. "You know that's not true."

"I do not know any such thing," Estelle said.

"The girls came over here on their own, Estelle, just as always. They've been coming over here since they could walk."

"It's because you tempt them over there. Then you use them like maids."

"They choose to come over here, Estelle, because they feel safe. Wouldn't you say that they need somewhere to feel safe?"

Estelle didn't answer her.

"Would you like me to send them back to you?"

This was unfair, Margot knew; she had no intention of sending the girls back. But Estelle had been unfair to her, too.

"No," Estelle said.

"Okay, then. You just let me know when you want them to come back. You know it's always a pleasure for me to have them."

They looked like trick-or-treaters: Darla wore a blue pin-striped, button-down, Brooks Brothers shirt Arlene had bought Jimmy before they were married, and a pair of Jimmy's blue jeans that, even rolled up, still hid her feet, so it seemed that she walked on stilts; Cara, too skinny for Jimmy's clothes, wore a horrid Brooks Brothers tartan smock, burnt-yellow, dried blood, and charcoal black, absurdly expensive, which Arlene also bought Margot before she was pregnant, which Margot had always loathed, but at the sight of which Cara's eyes widened in wonder. Her son, of course, had to get into the act, putting on Margot's old plush Kelly-green housecoat, with its vaguely regal cream and leopard-print trim, in which he used to parade around the house like a pasha.

Buddy and the girls hadn't spent this much time together since he'd started going with Jimmy on weekends, a year before. Cara and Darla sometimes hung around her house while Buddy was with Jimmy, or appeared briefly after school; but nothing like this, like the days before Jimmy returned, when they had all but lived there.

After she decided on what they would have for lunch—melting ice cream, omelets to use the eggs and cheese; and after she was sure the children were occupied with play that had not been so peaceful for many years—*her children*, she could not help but think, safe in her house—she turned to the built-in desk in the kitchen, piled with papers in stacks seemingly ragged and chaotic but in fact arranged according to a precise system known only to herself, to accomplish now, in an hour or two, if she were lucky, what she had planned would take all day. The laundry, even if the machines had been working, a lost cause; the dishes could be delegated to Buddy and the girls; likewise, cleaning the bathroom and sweeping the floors.

What was left, buried on her desk, was the letter from the lawyer. She didn't want to read it again. She didn't want to even look at it. Her lawyer that she couldn't afford told her Jimmy didn't have a case, but she could spend a lot of money fighting him, money she didn't have. Jimmy made more money now as a pathologist than she would ever see teaching medical technology.

This was Jimmy's proposal: He would buy a house in West University. Buddy would live there during the week. Margot would have him on weekends. Arlene already paid for him to go to private school. If the boy lived with

Jimmy during the week, Arlene said, he would be closer to the right children, the children at his school. It was a chance to give him a leg up in life, she said. It would be selfish of Margot to resist.

None of this was Jimmy's idea, of course. It was Arlene's. Arlene couldn't stand it, that Margot had seduced her son, dragged him into scandal, then abandoned him.

Margot hadn't planned on getting pregnant. Arlene suggested giving Buddy up for adoption. No one, not even Margot's own mother, thought it was a good idea for Margot, a single woman nearing forty, to have a child. Jimmy had insisted on marriage. But Jimmy, it turned out, had no real interest in being married. He had hated it, in fact, and took his rage at being trapped out on her. He'd never hit her; he'd needled and insulted and cheated on her. He hadn't even had the guts to properly leave her. When Buddy was seven, Jimmy went to Detroit for his residency, then into the Army, blaming her for not following him—absurd, she'd thought, a Hobson's choice, after how he'd treated her, that she would leave her house, her job, her mother in Houston, and follow him.

But Jimmy and Arlene were right. She'd allowed her loneliness and her arrogance to get the better of her—her loneliness, the years of working in the lab to pay for her parents' house; her arrogance, thinking she could use Jimmy to cure her loneliness.

How should she answer? If she let Buddy live with him, Jimmy would pay off her house, pay his expenses, still pay her support. It would mean the difference between retiring at sixty-five or working well into her seventies.

Darla was calling for her, her voice pitched at a level

of alarm that seemed to require Margot's actual presence. Buddy had been screaming and carrying on, but it hadn't been noteworthy enough for her to take action. He was always acting, always melodramatic.

In the hallway outside the bathroom, Darla stood, wringing her hands, her round beautiful face and quick blue eyes lit with alarm, and excitement.

"She's killing Beau!" she said. "She's killing him!"

For a moment, Margot couldn't trust what she saw. At first, she thought it was part of her son's movie. In the dimly lit bathroom, Cara knelt, mantis-like, over the toilet, in the horrid tartan dress. She was sick, Margot thought; then she imagined Cara was pregnant, and felt a bolt of panic. Then she saw Buddy, beneath Cara, stripped to his underwear, headless, because Cara was shoving his head into the toilet.

"What are you doing?" she said, pushing past Darla.

"He started running around and screaming and took off all his clothes," Cara said. "You don't do that, you hear?" she said to Buddy.

"Let him up!" Margot barked.

Cara pulled him up by his hair. Her son lolled back against Cara, sliding down into her lap, so that she had to kneel to hold him up. His eyes were closed; a faint, sated smile flickered on his lips, as if he were asleep and dreaming. Cara cradled his head against her stomach. Margot didn't know what to think.

"Have you lost your mind?" she said to Cara. "There are parasites in toilets."

"He was running around in his underwear," Cara said.

"He is still in his underwear," Margot said. "So you

have not improved the situation. I should send you both back home. Is that what you'd like?"

Cara, blushing, shrank from her. Margot felt guilty, playing this gambit; but she was angry with Cara for letting things get out of control. "Why on Earth were you running around in your underwear?" she asked.

"They wanted me to," he said, dreamily.

"What do you mean?" she said, poking him. "Did they ask you to?"

"No," he said, opening his eyes. "But I could tell."

"If they had wanted you to do that, they would have asked you."

"I wanted it to be like it was before," he said, telling a tale, spinning a yarn; he could rationalize anything, she thought, just like his father. "I used to run around naked all the time and no one minded. Now you like them better than me."

She wanted to tell him that at twelve years old, he was past the age to be acting this way; but she didn't see any point in humiliating him further.

"I like you just fine," she said. "It's not like it was before. Now clean up while there's still hot water. And put some clothes on."

While her son cleaned himself up, and the girls made lunch, Margot briefed them on the work that afternoon. She would enlist Buddy, too, to keep him out of trouble. Since Jimmy had started taking him on weekends, he had reverted to behavior he hadn't exhibited in years, tantrums that lasted hours, black moods that stretched for days. She didn't know what was wrong with him.

They ate lunch in the dim kitchen at the steel-topped

lab table Jimmy had salvaged from the old lab. The house hadn't gotten as hot as she'd expected, drawing up the cool air underneath it through the wooden floors; but a thin, sticky film of moisture clung to everything. The girls' faces were shiny with sweat. Margot wanted a glass of wine, but it was too early. There was still far too much to do. The backyard resembled a lake, lapping the shore of the concrete slab porch underneath the second story on Mr. Knight's house, reaching dangerously close to the side door of her garage. Someone would have to go outside to clear the drain.

The girls now gazed upon Buddy with sisterly compassion. By some mysterious means, a score had been settled between them, peace regained. Darla, in prosecutorial mode, recounted the horrors he had fed them about the private school Arlene paid for him to attend—the uniforms, the French lessons, the marching to chapel. Cara moued and nodded. Her son sat back in his chair, fattening like a tick on their sympathy.

"Beau told us he has to go over to his grand-mother's house every weekend," Darla said. "He says that he has to do all his schoolwork over again. He says that his grandmother's mean and crazy."

Margot shot a glance at him, piqued; he knew she didn't like him talking about their family. But of course, that was why he'd done it. He stared back at her, as cold-eyed as a gangster.

"She has been very generous to us," Margot said, hoping to convey by her tone that they had overstepped.

"Beau says he hates his school. He says it's full of snobs," Darla said, drawing out the long "ah" in "snobs."

Cara giggled.

"I hate it," he said.

"Why can't he go to Jackson?" Darla said.

Jackson was the public school down the street. Her son couldn't go to Jackson, Margot thought, because it was a war zone.

"Because he's going to St. Edward's," she said; then, to him, "Do you want to go to Jackson?"

"Sure," he said.

If faced with the actual prospect of going to Jackson, Margot knew, Buddy would beg not to; or if he went, he would get beaten up, bullied, or worse. She had moved fourteen times before graduating high school, and she'd gone to schools like Jackson, and she was not going to send her son to one, not if she could help it.

"Beau says his grandmother thinks he ought not to play with us," Darla said, staring dead at Margot with her beautiful blue eyes.

It was a question, Margot realized, that Darla wanted answered for the sake of her dignity—that was how Buddy had gotten the girls so riled up about Arlene, by implying that Arlene's sending him to St. Edward's was a sign of her disapproval of them. Which, of course, it was. He grinned at her vindictively.

"I'm sure she never said anything like that," Margot said, a hint.

"Yes, she did," her son said. "You know what she says about them. You know why she doesn't want me to play with them. She says they're trash."

Cara and Darla flinched as if they'd been struck. Margot saw he hadn't said this to them before. She wanted to reach across the table and slap him. He smirked at her, thinking only, she knew, of how pleased he was that he'd embarrassed her, not caring how his words hurt the girls. What would become of him? she thought. He was weak, like his father, seeking comfort wherever he could find it. She didn't know how she had raised such a child.

"You're right," she said. "I don't like you. Not when you act like this. You think you're so clever, but you're not. You're behaving like an imbecile."

Now it was Buddy's turn to flinch, his eyes to water. The girls looked at her curiously; she hoped they would remember that they could speak to a man like this. "No one's trash," she said. "Except people who call people trash. We're not going to talk about this anymore. We have a lot to do. Old Beau here is going to clear the drain."

Her son mumbled that she had told Jimmy the drain was just fine; but only a little. He knew he needed to redeem himself, Margot thought.

He changed into his yellow swimming trunks and went outside. The rain was still coming down hard. The girls and she watched from her bedroom, which had a view of both the yard and the street, where the drain reached the curb. After Jimmy had returned from the Army, when it was clear he wouldn't live with them anymore, he'd dug a trench through the yard to the curb, smashing the sidewalk and the curb with a sledgehammer to lay the drain pipe, then repaired the curb at the mouth of the drain and poured a new square of cement in the sidewalk. Later, she saw he had written their names in the sidewalk, and the year, 1977. Three years ago. It seemed like a lifetime. It would be out there forever, she thought, on her property, a

71

monument to folly, a tombstone; sometimes, she imagined going outside and smashing it, as well.

They watched Buddy wade into the yard, squinting in the rain, his hair plastered dark and slick on his head, his yellow swimming trunks plastered against his sex. He moved carefully through the water, carrying a garbage bag, his face grave and older-looking; she had instructed him to put the detritus from the drain into the bag, wait for the drain to clog, then clear it again. She imagined lightning hitting the pecan tree, or the metal fence, water moccasins and amoebic waterborne diseases. If anything happened to him, how would she explain it to Jimmy and Arlene?

Then, she thought, he was hers to sacrifice, if she wanted. If Abraham could take Isaac to the mountain, why couldn't she send her son to unclog a drain? She had fought, first to have him, then to keep him. He was and would always be hers.

Her son cleared muck out of the drain into the bag, then waited. A whirlpool formed, drawing in more sticks and leaves and who knew what else; he cleared it again. Margot watched him, and the mouth of the drain at the street; it was possible the pipe had clogged, and all of this would be for naught. Cara and Darla were following the drama, too, remembering how Jimmy put in the drain— the story of the sledgehammer and the new concrete. The boy stood over the drain in the yard, waiting. In his frowning, abstracted face, she saw Jimmy's face, and the faces of her father, her uncles, her cousins, silent, dutiful men—useful men.

In the street, a gout of leaves and dirt pulsed into the water rushing past it, toward the storm drain. In the yard, water spun, disappearing around her son's ankles. In Margot's house, she and the girls cheered.

The children worked hard, cleaning the house, even after Buddy had cleared the drain. Margot made them a dinner of salad and pork chops pan-fried on the gas stove, and the rest of the ice cream, which they drank from wine glasses. Tomorrow, if the power didn't return, she would have to start throwing out milk and meat from the freezer. Though it was still light outside, the kitchen was dark; they sat at the steel-topped table and ate in silence in the dark room. Then she and Buddy stood on the back stoop, watching the girls pick their way across the paving stones, through the gate between the yards that was always open, still wearing the clothes she had given them. They didn't turn to wave goodbye; they had already entered the world where they really lived.

She and Buddy found the hurricane candles in a kitchen drawer and lit them on the dining room table and in the kitchen. She had a glass of wine and the house took on a honeyed glow. The steel-topped table and the furniture in the living room and their own faces, as they carried the candles from room to room, were reflected on the windows, so that it looked as if, outside, some other version of themselves lived beyond the house, in a world of holy silence.

She imagined the girls in Mr. Knight's dark house, burrowing into piles of clothes or under their beds in the close, foul-smelling maze of rooms in the house's upper story. She hoped Cara would stay with Darla, to protect her, that Estelle would remain vigilant. Each night, she prayed to the Virgin to intercede, though she knew this was not enough. She knew that she herself had not done enough to protect them.

In the candlelit kitchen, she and Buddy were safe.

"I wish it could always be like this," she said.

"Like what?" he said.

"Just the two of us," she said, worried that she had admitted too much.

"Then why do you make me go over there?"

"Because he is your father, and Grandmother is your grandmother, and they have been very kind and generous."

"That's bullshit," he said. "You're just doing it for the money. And because you're too weak to stand up to him. You're weak, weak, weak."

"Please, honey," she said.

"Bullshit, bullshit, bullshit, bullshit," he said, prodding her arm.

"Enough," she said. "If you don't want to go over there, why don't you tell Grandmother you don't want to go over there? You can't do that, can you?"

He turned from her, his fists clenched, his head bowed. In the shifting light, his face looked as it had when he was very young.

"I'm sorry, honey," she said. "I'm sorry."

He took one of the candles from the table and carried it to his room, where he spent most of his time, now, working on his movie, he said. The glow of his candle wavered through the dining room, around the corner into the hallway. She wanted to follow him, but knew it would do no good, now, to try to talk to him.

Soon, she would have to call her mother. She braced herself with Ritz crackers and a second glass of wine, still raw with shame and anger at what she had said. She regretted her anger and having lost her temper and letting Buddy gain the upper hand by making her lose her temper; she regretted having married and having bought her house and having kept her son, and then she was horrified by the self-indulgence of her regret. She couldn't run, as she had last summer on their trip across Texas, trying to escape it. She couldn't think of how she had kept letting Jimmy into her house, into her bed, long after she knew he wouldn't come back. There was no way out of the mess that she had made of her life except through it, no other way out of the poison of her regret.

The line rang so many times she began to worry that her mother had fallen. She had no idea if the streets were clear enough to even get to her house. She imagined the embarrassment of calling Mr. Torres, asking him to look in.

She knew what her mother would say, when she told her that Jimmy hadn't come. Margot had made the mistake of telling her about Buddy's tantrums when he came home from his Saturdays with Jimmy, his rages that lasted through Mass the next morning and into the week. Her mother had said his visits with Jimmy were ruining him.

But what did her mother know about real life? What did she know about working or paying off a house? Margot had bought the house for them when she started working at the lab in college, because by then her father was too ill to work, and her mother had never worked a day in her life. All her mother knew about was her books. Margot had done what she had needed to do. She could do nothing, now, except what she had been doing, giving the girls a place to stay, fighting Arlene inch by inch.

Her mother answered. She had been in another part of the house, she said. Her power was out? Yes, her power was out; but Mr. Torres had stopped by to check in on her, and Mrs. Roberts had called, and so had Hazel Rosen and Annette Quine. It was exhausting. And how was her day? Did Jimmy come over in all this mess? Margot said he hadn't; Buddy had stayed home.

"And how was that?" her mother asked.

"It was wonderful," Margot said, surprised, and a little ashamed, by the outsized, melodramatic word. But it was true; the day had been wonderful.

Tickle Torture

Since they left Houston that summer, Buddy and his mother had traveled in a long, slow circuit as far north as Amarillo, then worked their way down through El Paso and San Antonio and Austin, seeing sights Buddy had no desire to see, and in which he doubted his mother had any real interest, either. For a month, he had collected brochures in the bottom of his duffel bag. They had visited: the Alamo, the Helium Monument, Dinosaur Valley, Prairie Dog Town, the National Mule Memorial, Fort Phantom Hill, The Cave Without A Name, Pioneertown, and the Tarantula Railroad, as well as museums—the Dr. Pepper Museum, the Santa Claus Museum, the Texas Prison Museum, the Border Patrol Museum, the Confederate Air Force Museum, the Jim Reeves Memorial, and the Buddy Holly Statue and Walk of Fame.

Currently, they were near Galveston, on their way to

see the third oldest ship afloat. It didn't really matter where they went; his mother looked through everything, as if she did not quite know where she was. Buddy wondered whether she had kept her job at the hospital, and how they were paying for the trip, and when if ever they would go to Corpus. He didn't want to go back to Houston, where his father still haunted their house like a ghost.

Each summer, even after his father had gone to Detroit, then Fort Polk, Buddy and his parents had visited Corpus Christi where his cousins Cecilia and Amien lived. Aunt Beatrice, their mother, was his father's sister. This year Buddy's mother said she didn't want to deal with Aunt Beatrice and all the questions she would ask.

In their motel room near Galveston his mother brushed her teeth and washed her face, chiding his father in the mirror. To keep from listening Buddy turned on the TV; the voice his mother used in the mirror had nothing to do with anything she'd said to his father since he'd come back to Houston, but hadn't lived with them.

Buddy changed into swimming trunks and a T-shirt, noticing, even in the room's dim light, how dirty they were. He propped himself up against the headboard and tried to remember the last time his mother had washed his clothes.

As usual, they were sharing a room because his mother wanted to economize. When there was only one bed, like now, some motel clerks offered to set up cots, but most didn't bother.

Buddy thought about Cecilia and Amien, whose father had died the previous summer. In past summers, Buddy and his cousins had snuck out, dressed as witches and gypsies, to tell each other secrets while their parents slept.

But when Buddy and his parents had gone to their father's funeral, his cousins had hardly spoken to him. He hoped that this year, if he could persuade his mother to go, they could sneak out, as they always had before.

His mother glided past the TV. One minute, Mary Tyler Moore was there, then a silhouette of his mother's plump body. Her nightgowns were blue and thin; they seemed made not of fabric, but of smell: a warm, sweet odor of cold cream and sweat and flesh. She raised the stiff bedcovers and settled herself next to him.

"I still don't see why we can't go," he said.

"Please, honey." His mother lay her hand across her forehead and shut her eyes. "We've been over this a thousand times."

"If daddy was here, we'd go." Buddy said this not because he believed it, but to nettle her. "Everything was better when daddy was around. We didn't drive all day and see boring things and stay in crummy motels. We were normal."

His mother shielded her eyes. "The sun was brighter, the sky bluer, and you never had to go to school."

"That's right."

"We floated through life on a pink perfumed cloud."

Buddy laughed, but his throat ached, as it did when he cried.

"A pink perfumed cloud," his mother said, glancing at him, tweaking his armpit.

Laughing, he squirmed away from her. It didn't feel like it used to, when they sat on her bed, eating animal crackers and watching TV, waiting for his father to call from Detroit, or Fort Polk. Then, tickling had been a kind of relief. Now, it felt as if his mother were trying to make him believe he was happy. She noodled his ribs, and he batted her hands away.

"Honey," she said. "What's wrong?"

"I told you."

"Do you really want to go?"

"I told you," he said, hiding his face from her.

He lay with his head in her lap. She stroked his hair until he shook off her hand. Since his father had come back, Buddy often slept with her, as he had when he was very young. He knew that most eleven-year-old boys didn't cry on their mothers' laps, or sleep with them, or allow themselves to be tickled, but he hadn't told any of the boys at school what his life was like with his mother. That was why he wanted to go to Corpus.

His mother got up to turn off the TV. When she lay down, Buddy listened to her breath slow and deepen. Streetlight bled across the ceiling above the room's sole window. He tried to dream of Cecilia and Amien. He saw them as they had been at their father's funeral: They wore dark satin dresses, their eyes downcast, their mouths tightly shut.

Toward dawn, sunlight peeked through the curtains. Buddy woke to find himself pressed against his mother's back. Carefully, he propped himself up and drew back the covers. He studied her soft, sleeping, mysterious body, then covered her before she woke.

That morning, his mother told him they could go to

Corpus. After they ate at a diner across the parking lot from their motel, she found a pay phone and loaded it with coins. Every few days, she called his grandmother, his father's mother, to tell her where they were. Buddy looked for the name of the motel, so he could tell his cousins where he'd been, but all the sign said was "Motel."

"Hello, Bea?" his mother said. "Oh, Cecilia? How are you, darling? Could you put your mother on?"

The day was bright and hazy, already hot. Eighteen-wheelers moaned in the distance, then flashed past on the interstate, making rattletrap noises. His mother blinked in the flat white sunlight, as if for the first time on their trip she had woken up, and didn't particularly like what she saw. She wore a rumpled sacklike denim dress and work shoes. Her hair, which was threaded with gray, had outgrown its sensible cut. Though shadowed and lined by fatigue, her face was full and delicate, still beautiful in his eyes.

"Bea?" she said. "This is Margot. We're fine. He's right here." She glared at him. "He wants to visit the girls. I'm sorry this is such short notice. We probably won't stay long." She held the receiver against her chest, then spoke into it. "It's very kind of you, Bea. We'll see you soon.

"I hope you appreciate this," she said to him when she hung up.

Late that afternoon, they parked in front of Aunt Beatrice's house. The car shuddered, sighed, ticked in the heat. Buddy kept his eyes on a monster magazine. Three vampire girls, their hair long and blonde, their eyes feline, sauntered through the archway of a crypt. "We're here," his mother said.

If Buddy looked closely, he could see through the vampire girls' blood-stained dresses. "The Daughters of Lilith bleed their victims dry," ran the caption. "But do these hapless lovers feel pleasure, or pain—or both?!—at the hands of Satan's concubine?"

"Let's go," said his mother, looking at his magazine. "What is this? Where'd you get it? Put it away. You don't want Beatrice to see it."

When he didn't move, she said, "What's wrong, honey?"

"I don't know."

"What do you mean you don't know?"

Her question rankled him. "I don't know."

His mother reached for his armpit, then glanced at Aunt Beatrice's neat suburban box. Buddy shrank against the passenger door. "If you don't get out of this car on the count of five," she said, "we're going turn right around and go back."

"Fine," said Buddy.

His mother stuck the key in the ignition, then seemed to deflate. "Dammit, honey. What're you going to do, sit out here?"

"I might."

"And what am I supposed to tell Beatrice?"

"I don't care. Tell her I died."

Glowering at him, his mother got out and slammed her door. Buddy watched her disappear behind an azalea bush that hid Aunt Beatrice's porch. A string stretched tight in his chest, but he did not follow her; he looked at his magazine. Its back cover, which advertised magic kits and mind-reading courses, was torn from its stapled spine. A boy at school named Sam Fahr had lent it to him. Sam's father had also left. Sometimes Sam's mother let his father spend the night, and Sam described to Buddy the noises that came from her room. Sam and Buddy agreed that vampire girls, if they existed, wouldn't let men treat them as their fathers had their mothers. All summer, Buddy had imagined himself and Cecilia and Amien as vampire girls, marauding through the streets, then curling into a crypt, their bodies slick with gore. Now, in front of Aunt Beatrice's house, he was afraid to show them the pictures. But he was more afraid that Aunt Beatrice would see them if she came to get him. He left his magazine in the car and approached the house.

Before he could knock, the front door opened with an air-conditioned sigh. Amien peeked out from behind it. She was a year younger than Buddy, three years younger than Cecilia; a flouncy white dress covered a body as plump and awkward as his own. Her eyes, in her round, pale face, were dark, lustrous, and mean.

"Where've you been?" she said. "There's something on your shirt."

Blushing, Buddy looked down and scratched at a splotch of mustard.

"I guess you should come in." Amien paused, holding the door ajar. "Cecilia and I have important things to do. Cecilia and I are allergic to dust."

Wondering if his cousins had always been allergic to dust, Buddy entered a dim, familiar hallway. The house was hushed, as if everyone in it were waiting and hidden.

Amien slipped behind him to close the door, then stood close, studying him. "Our mothers are fighting in the kitchen," she said. "My mother says your mother's insane."

Buddy's heart sank. "Can we sneak out tonight?"

Amien's eyes narrowed. "We don't play those kind of games anymore." She walked briskly down the hallway and vanished into her room.

Buddy stood in the dim hallway. The house seemed to watch him. He ran to the kitchen and burst through its door. Aunt Beatrice and his mother turned, their mouths opened and eyes wide, but he did not stop until he clung to his mother's waist.

"Stop that," his mother said, pulling him away. But he knew she would have gathered him into her soft lap if they had been alone.

"Look what you've done to him," Aunt Beatrice said.

Buddy faced her, ready to show his aunt that nothing was wrong.

Sheathed in a pink housecoat as stiff and quilted as an oven mitt, Aunt Beatrice crouched in front of him, steadying herself on his shoulders. Her skin looked hollow, as if her insides had been dissolved by a wasting disease. She examined him with eyes darker, yet kinder, than Amien's. "How are you, my little man?" she said.

Buddy said that he was fine.

"You don't look so fine to me. Did something frighten you?"

"No," he said.

Aunt Beatrice frowned. "Do you always miss your mother this much?"

His mother laid her hand on the nape of his neck. "He's tired."

Aunt Beatrice neither moved nor took her eyes from him. Her eyes were close; they seemed to almost touch him. "You're not very talkative," she said. "You're not the bright little talkative man you used to be. Now why do you think that is?"

"I don't know," he said.

She rose, pressing his shoulders. "Would you like to go to the beach tomorrow?"

Buddy looked at his mother, who bit her lip. He asked Aunt Beatrice if his cousins were going; she said they were. Though he was afraid, Buddy said that he would go, too.

That night, Buddy lay next to his mother on a fold-out bed in the parlor. She kept her back to him, but he could tell by her breathing that she was awake. He looked at the ceiling, where leaves tousled by the night wind cast quivering shadows. Aunt Beatrice had set up a cot next to the bed. In summers past, he'd slept on a trundle in Cecilia's room, but this year, Aunt Beatrice had taken his duffel bag to the parlor and told him he would sleep there. His cousins had refused to even come to dinner.

"Buddy," his mother said. "Are you awake?"

Buddy said that he was.

"I'm sorry about the girls. Maybe we should just leave."

"But we're going to the beach tomorrow."

After a pause, his mother said, "You know why

Beatrice wants you to go to the beach. She wants you to see how fun it is to live here."

His mother wasn't usually so concerned with what he thought. "That's not true."

She rolled over, her face red and convulsed. Buddy thought of a fat boy at school named Billy Flagg, whom the other boys teased each day until he cried. Sometimes, Buddy teased him, too. "I always knew daddy was going to leave," she said. "But I've never felt that way with you. I never want to lose you."

As he had many times since his father left, Buddy drew his mother to himself, and felt her warm breath against his chest, and her body quake against his own.

"I won't leave," he said, hoping no one could hear them.

The next morning, Buddy did not look at his mother. Before she woke, he went to a bright yellow bathroom, where a mirror covered a wall above a pair of sinks. He turned on the shower and undressed, then tucked his private parts between his legs, wishing his cousins could see him from the mirror's other side.

When he returned to the parlor, his mother was gone, so he went to the kitchen door. His aunt's voice was like a sewing machine. She had called his grandmother, and had some questions: Had his mother kept her job? Did she know where Buddy was going to go to school that fall? Did she have a destination? His mother said she didn't know.

"You don't know much of anything, do you?" Aunt

Beatrice said.

"I guess I don't," said his mother. "I guess you've got it all figured out."

"Maybe I've got it figured better than you. It's been four years since Jimmy left; you need to start pulling things together, if not for yourself, at least for that poor child."

"What do you think I've been doing? I get up and go to work and go to sleep and do it all over again. I feel like I'm not even human."

"It doesn't matter how you feel. Do you think it's been easy for me since David's gone? At least my brother's still alive."

"I'm not going back to Houston," his mother said.

"I'm not saying you should," said his aunt. "I think you should stay here."

Before his mother could answer, Buddy opened the door. Aunt Beatrice turned to him, holding a large knife. On the counter next to her were cubes of cantaloupe and plastic bags. She had exchanged her pink housecoat for a purple muumuu printed with trumpet-shaped flowers. His mother still wore her denim dress.

"There you are," Aunt Beatrice said, as if Buddy had been hiding from her. She told him to take the beach chairs and umbrella out of the garage and load them into his uncle's station wagon. "It shouldn't be a problem," she said. "You're a big, strong man."

His mother smiled at him, but her smile was distant and sad.

In the back of the station wagon, Buddy grappled with an umbrella and beach chairs, remembering how his uncle and father had tossed them to each other from the garage. His father caught them easily, but his uncle flinched, like a girl afraid of a baseball. Corpus had been different, then. His mother, though timid with his father, had kept Buddy in line with merely a glance.

His uncle had died in a car crash in Amarillo. Sometimes, Buddy wished his father had come to just as definite an end. He had never been around much, and now he wasn't exactly gone. He stayed with his girlfriend, Mary Winifreed, but his shirts and ties still hung in Buddy's mother's closet, and sometimes, he still spent the night with his mother. Buddy knew it was not his father's absence, but his ghostly reappearances, which were driving his mother crazy.

Buddy felt someone watching him. Through a smudged window in the back of the station wagon, he saw, standing on the porch, a long-limbed girl with golden hair, whom he did not recognize at first as Cecilia.

They drove through winding streets, past identical houses, until they reached the beachfront road. There, the houses looked like abandoned movie sets, their pink adobe façades cracked and peeling. Dead palm trees swayed landward over the road.

In the front seat, Aunt Beatrice and his mother were silent. Buddy sat between his cousins in the back. Amien was pressed against her door, scowling at him. Her eyes weren't as mean as they had been in the house, but Buddy no longer cared.

He furtively studied Cecilia. Her face glowed with a

vague, hazy film that Buddy had noticed on older girls. She stared out her window, far away, as if she could not be bothered with where she was.

The palm trees disappeared and the flimsy houses were replaced with skittering fields of brush. "The beaches in town aren't safe anymore," Aunt Beatrice said.

When they parked on a desolate shoulder paved with oyster shells, the sun was high and blinding. Cecilia and Amien tore out of the car and ran toward the beach, leaving the rest of them to unpack. After the chairs were set out, the umbrella planted, and a red cooler unloaded, Buddy's mother rubbed sunscreen on him; he twisted away from her.

Cecilia and Amien returned to shed their T-shirts and shorts. Both wore blue, one-piece bathing suits. When Cecilia bent to pick a handful of plastic bags out of the cooler, Buddy glimpsed the cleft between her breasts, and felt a hollow ache.

"Remember, girls," Aunt Beatrice said. "Don't walk past the pier."

Without acknowledging her, they raced back to the beach, harsh laughter trailing behind them. Buddy hesitated. "Go on," his mother said, in the voice she used in the mirror with his father. "This is what you came for."

Uncertain of what she meant, though cut by her tone, he started after them. Aunt Beatrice clasped his arm. "Keep an eye on them, my little man."

Without meeting her eyes, Buddy nodded until she let him go. As he neared the ocean, seaweed, dead fish, and tar overwhelmed the babyish scent of his sunscreen.

Ahead, Cecilia tossed cubes of cantaloupe to chattering

gulls, who swooped above the tidal water, then settled into their awkward, land-bound gaits. She walked as if she watched herself in a secret mirror. Amien picked her way through broken bottles and bits of Styrofoam, scampering toward her sister with a gull's mincing steps.

Afraid to come closer, Buddy slowed his pace. Cecilia stopped and turned to him. "We're going to see some friends of mine," she said. "My mother doesn't know about them. If you tell on us, I'll strip you naked and lock you outside the house tonight."

Amien nodded sternly, arms folded over her stomach. His cousins walked on, and Buddy fell in beside them. He wanted them to himself.

"What's it like, living with your mom?" Cecilia asked him.

"It's okay," he said cautiously.

"Our mother's crazy. The only place she takes us is this crappy beach." Cecilia's eyes focused on a distant point. "D'you know about Janis Joplin? I'd give anything to live on the road like she did. Rick told me about getting high with her."

"Who's Rick?" said Buddy, but Cecilia didn't answer.

Ahead loomed the pier, whose planks had mostly vanished, leaving a line of bare pilings to march into the waves. His cousins stopped behind one of them. Buddy could see the pulse in Cecilia's neck, and her blue bathing suit flutter over her heart.

In a clearing in the scrub brush beyond the pier was a rough circle of cars, and men and women leaning on their hoods. The men wore cut-off jeans and concert T-shirts, the women, some not much older than Cecilia, bikini tops and jeans cut shorter than the men's. Buddy had seen such people before, on beaches and in the parking lots of malls. Sam Fahr's older brother was one of them. He flashed a switchblade so swiftly that Buddy had never actually seen it; he only knew it was there enough to be afraid.

"Someone's with him," said Amien.

"I got eyes," Cecilia said.

"What're you going to do?"

"I'm gonna talk to him." She looked at them. "I ain't got nothing to be ashamed of."

Cecilia walked slowly toward the cars. Amien let out a stifled cry, then covered her mouth with her hand. The people glanced at Cecilia. A man and woman, older than the rest, watched her closely. The man was tall and thin, the woman's face as hard and still as a mask. The man hoisted himself up from the hood of his car and approached Cecilia. A thick gray ponytail swung from the back of his head.

"Who's that?" Buddy said.

"It's Rick," said Amien, as if Rick were someone he should know.

When Rick stopped close to Cecilia, Buddy saw how small she was. Then Rick brushed her hair from her face and let his hand settle on the nape of her neck, and Buddy clenched his fists, his imagination bloody and heroic. Cecilia did not move. The woman turned to the people, who looked away.

"Is he Cecilia's boyfriend?" Buddy asked.

"No," said Amien, her dark eyes riveted. "Of course not."

Rick spoke to Cecilia, though they couldn't hear him,

then brought his face close to hers. She shook her head, like a horse refusing a bridle, and ran toward the pier.

By then, the people had noticed Buddy and Amien. Rick lumbered toward them. They ran. Amien clutched Buddy's hand, but let go of it when they neared Cecilia.

She wheeled on them, her face red, as his mother's had been the night before; but Buddy felt none of the revulsion for her that he had for his mother.

"I ain't got nothing to be ashamed of," she said to him. "Understand?"

"Yes," he said, though he didn't.

"'You're my little girl,'" she said to Amien, her voice bitter. "That's what he said to me. Then he tried to kiss me, right there in front of his girlfriend."

Amien stared at her.

"You better not tell anyone," Cecilia said to Buddy. "I swear if you breathe a word, I'll do worse than what I told you."

"I won't," he said. He thought: I will never hurt you.

"I know what he's thinking," she said to Amien. "He wants to make her jealous. But I'm not gonna hang around just so they can laugh at me."

Amien nodded, her eyes vacant and frightened.

"He's like my father," said Buddy.

Amien looked at him as if she wished he would disappear; Cecilia's gaze was sharp and searching.

"If we sneak out tonight," he said. "I'll tell you all about him."

Amien turned away from him, but Cecilia said, "Maybe."

When they returned to Aunt Beatrice's house, his cousins disappeared, and Buddy went to the bathroom, to avoid his aunt and mother. He showered, not looking at himself in the mirror. An image haunted him: Rick bent over Cecilia, his wiry body enveloping her, his ponytail on his bare back, pendulous and obscene.

After showering, he went to his uncle's study, more dim and still than the rest of the house. Gilt lettering glimmered on bookcases in the wood-paneled gloom. He touched a pair of reading glasses on his uncle's desk and felt a queasy shock.

He remembered his uncle lifting him to pluck oranges from a tree in the back yard. His hands had been gentle, his smile friendly, and Buddy had wished that he were his father.

"There you are," Aunt Beatrice said.

She stood very close to him. In the room's pale light, her face was thinned almost to transparency. She asked him what he and his cousins had done at the beach, and he told her they had talked about Janis Joplin.

Buddy lay on the cot in the parlor, watching leaf-shadows sway across the ceiling, hoping that his cousins would come. At dinner, they sat mutely through Aunt Beatrice's interrogation, then retreated without a word to him. Buddy wished he had told on them, to protect them from

93

Rick, to punish them for not coming, to insure that at least they would throw him out of the house naked. That might be easier than telling them about his father; he had told no one about him, not even Sam Fahr.

"Buddy?" his mother said. "Are you there?"

Buddy debated whether to answer. "Yes," he said.

"I want to leave. Your aunt means well, but she's driving me crazy."

Buddy said nothing. His mother turned under the covers, and her scent breathed into the room. Buddy lay rigid, arms at his sides, furiously wishing she would sleep.

"Why don't you come over here so we can talk?" she said.

"I can hear you just fine from where I am."

After a pause, she said, "I'm scared, Buddy. Won't you please come here?"

Buddy closed his eyes. His mother's breath was shallow and quiet; she waited for him. When his father spent the night, he lay in bed, listening to her plead with his father to stay, and his father's murmurous answers, and his brutal grunts, and her thin cries. He knew what the sounds meant, and hated his father for hurting her, and his mother for letting him, and both of them for leaving it to him to comfort her. Now, as he listened to her breath slow and deepen, he knew that he was no better than his father.

"Come on," Cecilia whispered. She stood over him, her face close to his.

Heart racing, he followed her to the living room,

where she told him to wait until he heard his name, then slipped behind a wall of curtains. He stood in darkness, shadows gathering around him, then heard his name, like wind through a porch screen, and lifted an edge of the curtains and slowly slid open a glass door.

At the far end of the sunroom, his cousins sat in a circle of candles, which cast their wavering shadows on the screen windows and aluminum walls. They were draped in paisley dresses and flowing scarves; their faces looked masked and strange.

"Close the door," Cecilia said.

Fingers trembling, he slid the door closed, remembering how they had danced here while their parents slept, their faces white, lips blood-red, fingers bent like claws. He had told them he wanted to live with them, but he could not remember their secrets anymore.

"Come here," Cecilia said.

As he approached, he saw that his cousins' eyelids were green and purple, their lips a glistening pink, their faces dusted with sparkles. Amien's was pale and brooding, and Cecilia's seemed drained by its harsh colors. He wished that he were dressed like a gypsy, his face painted like theirs.

"Sit down," she said.

Buddy stepped over the candles, their flames tickling the soles of his feet, and sat cross-legged on the floor. The room disappeared behind the candlelight.

"We speak to the dead and tell the future and read people's minds," said Cecilia. "We're going to read yours, to see if you should live with us."

When he didn't answer, she pressed her fingers to her temples and fluttered her eyelids. "I hear your mother crying in my dreams."

"She misses your father," said Amien.

"She misses you." Cecilia stared at him. "She's afraid you'll run away and live with us. She's afraid of your father, 'cause he won't leave her alone."

A night breeze fluttered the candles, and his cousins' faces shifted. Buddy was frightened by how much they already knew, and how much they might not be saying.

"Tell me about Rick," he said.

"That's none of your business," said Amien.

His cheeks burned, and he looked away from them, but Cecilia leaned toward him. "Some nights," she said, "I meet him outside and we drive to the beach. They have bonfires. They're out there right now. I could go if I wanted."

The image of Rick's bare back returned. Buddy glanced at Amien, but she would not meet his eyes. "What do you do?" he asked Cecilia.

"What do you think we do?"

"I don't know."

"Really?" Cecilia smiled. "You don't know what people do?"

"I know." Buddy stopped, aware of the trap into which he'd fallen. His cousins studied him, their eyes curious and hooded.

"Then why don't you tell us?" Cecilia said.

If he told them to read his mind, their game would end. "My father's a vampire," he said. "He visits in the middle of the night. My mother cries when he feeds on her."

"That's a lie," Amien said to him.

"What does it sound like?" Cecilia asked, her face glittering, her stare intent.

He had no words for what it sounded like. Instead, he beat the floor, uttering high, sharp cries, until his fist was numb. Cecilia caught his hand, no longer smiling, and unfolded his fingers.

"Is it true?" Amien asked her.

"Of course it's true." Cecilia pressed his hand. "That's why his mother's crazy."

"He's lying," Amien said. "That's not what people sound like."

"How would you know?" Gripping Cecilia's hand, he leaned close to Amien. "Maybe I'm a vampire. Maybe I sneak into my mother's bed and drink her blood and look at her when she's naked."

Amien rose awkwardly, gathering her dress around her. "You're crazy," she said. "Just like your mother. You want to ruin everything with your sick stories."

"Be quiet," said Cecilia. "You're gonna get us in trouble."

"I don't care."

"Then leave." Cecilia didn't look at her. "Go to your room and be quiet."

Amien hovered over them. For a moment, Buddy thought she would scream, but she fled to the sliding doors.

"Is it true?" Cecilia said. "I mean, not really true, but true your dad comes around?"

He nodded, looking at their hands.

"Everything I told you about Rick is a lie. They have bonfires, but I've never even been to one."

"I knew that."

"You can't stay," she said. "Amien'll say something to my mom."

"I never said I wanted to stay."

"That's okay," she said. "I'm gonna leave, too. I can't right now, 'cause they'll just bring me home. But when I'm sixteen, they won't be able to do anything. Maybe then I'll come and get you."

Buddy knew she was lying. When he looked at her, though, he saw that she believed what she'd said. She pulled him up by his hand, and he could not help but feel dizzy and blessed. They blew out candles until it was dark, and then Cecilia was gone.

Before dawn, Buddy woke his mother and told her that he wanted to leave. While the house still slept, they packed their bags and snuck out to the car.

At sunrise, they tilted onto the Corpus Christi Bridge and rose into the air. Buddy looked down at the tiny scalloped waves below, and imagined the car spinning off the bridge and crashing into them. He wished it would happen. He had betrayed his mother for nothing. There was nowhere else to go.

He did not know that in a week, he and his mother would return to Houston. His mother would get her job at the hospital back and work overtime to pay off her credit cards. His father would appear less and less, though he would never entirely disappear. The summer before his first year of high school, Aunt Beatrice would call to tell his mother that Cecilia had run away, and Buddy would find himself waiting for her, though he knew she would never come. By then, he and his mother would move carefully around each other, spending their evenings in separate rooms, shutting their doors at bedtime. They mentioned their last trip to Corpus, when they mentioned it at all, as if it had happened to other people, people they didn't know.

But now they are in a motel somewhere in Texas. The room is cold and bright. His mother has just finished brushing her teeth and changing for bed. She glides past Buddy, who is sitting cross-legged on their bed, staring at the dead, green eye of the TV.

She lifts the covers and settles herself on a pillow against the headboard. Her scent wafts toward him; he tries to believe it is filthy. She dons a pair of glasses, opens a book, then lowers it. "What's gotten into you?" she says.

"Nothing."

"Are you still upset about Corpus?"

"No."

"I told you we shouldn't have gone. If you're upset, it's your own fault."

Buddy looks at her. Behind her reading glasses, her eyes are warped and peevish. "I'm not upset," he says to the TV. "And it's not my fault."

"Really? Whose fault is it?"

"It's your fault."

"I don't know what you mean," she says indignantly; but he knows she is afraid.

He turns to her. "You keep pretending like you don't know what I mean so you can keep acting crazy. But I'm not crazy. I'm not a freak. *You're* a big, fat freak and everyone can see it."

"What happened, honey?"

He looks away. In the TV, they are faceless, huddled shadows.

"Buddy?" she says. "Do you want a house like Aunt Beatrice's?"

"No."

"Do you want sisters like Cecilia and Amien?"

"No."

"Do you want another daddy?"

"No," he says, afraid of what he will say to her. "Leave me alone."

"Why, honey? What did I do? Please tell me what I did wrong."

She leans toward him, and he faces her. Her breasts sag against her nightgown; she sees him glance at them, and covers them with her arm.

"I don't want to be here," he says. "I haven't ever wanted to be with you."

"Am I really that bad?"

"Yes," Buddy says. But then he thinks: No, she's not. If she's that bad, then he is, too. But what he says is true enough, hurtful enough, for the moment. "Yes," he says again. "You really are."

Her eyes strain through her glasses. He cannot stand her eyes on him anymore.

Swiftly, he wiggles a finger into her plump armpit. She lets out a yelp, then yaws backward, trying to escape. She catches his ribs and he falls on her hand, but she tweaks him behind his knee. He springs like a doused cat. He wriggles and kicks, but here she comes. She has him now. She digs into his ribs and he screams, wondering if anyone can hear them, and if so, what they must think. He imagines how they must look in the dead, green eye of the TV: a plump boy wriggling beneath his half-naked mother, who giggles while she tickles him. He kicks the air. She tickles the soles of his feet. It is delicious, unbearable. He bats her hands from his chest, and they go under his arms, he bats them from there and they go under his knees, like a crazy, short-circuiting machine. Around and around go her hands, and his hands chase them. He clutches her arm, ready to beg mercy, but he will stay here just a moment longer. He writhes, gasps, thinking: this is not how it should be; thinking: I do not know how it should be.

Hester

Hester's uniform was always spotlessly clean and fresh-smelling. She smelled like a perfume kiosk at the mall. She wore a little mascara and a smudge of blue eyeliner to highlight her blue eyes. Her nose was a little too big to allow her plain oval face to be beautiful. She wasn't as pretty as she, Sarah, was—this wasn't conceit, Sarah thought, just a fact, one she sensed Hester register, as well. Unlike Sarah, at least how she'd dressed in high school, in ragged T-shirts, tie-dyed skirts and crumbling jeans, nothing about Hester was put on, nothing called attention to itself. But this, Sarah knew, was what made Hester so appealing to customers, both men and women, unlike she, Sarah, from whom they recoiled. Hester was country cute. She had a soothing way with the old folks, a maternal matter-of-factness with moms, and flirted chastely with the single men and teenage boys. She had an uncanny ability, Sarah observed, to intuit who at a table would be paying the bill, and targeted them.

Hester was a few years older than Sarah. Yet Hester still lived with her mother, a nurse who worked flexible shifts to help care for Hester's baby, whose name was Aanya, meaning gift from God. Hester had shown Sarah pictures of Aanya. Except for her ridiculous cowgirl getup of gingham shirt, denim overalls, and red bandana, Aanya looked like any other baby, Sarah thought. Then she felt a flash of rage—at the ridiculous costume, at the pride with which Hester spoke of Aanya, at Aanya's wide-eyed innocent gaze—before she recoiled from herself, horrified by her own anger.

The Pizza Hut was tucked behind a movie theater in the corner of a parking lot in a mall where half the stores were empty, on the other side of Robert Mueller Airport from the University, right next to I-35. When Sarah applied for the job, it had already been robbed twice. She knew this because she'd read about the robberies in *The Daily Texan*, and because Hester told her.

Hester didn't tell Sarah how it had felt to be robbed, or complain that the Pizza Hut Corporation refused to post police sketches of the robbers—a fact Sarah knew from the article in the *Texan*. Hester told her how to be safe: Don't argue with them, don't look them in the eye, just give them the money.

Sarah couldn't tell if Hester was mocking her, or trying to warn her. Hester's blond hair, pinned above her ears, cascaded down her neck in poodley rings; her dull blue eyes, the eyes of Bible thumpers and cheerleaders, glinted judgment and condemnation.

"You're a college girl," Hester said. "What are you doing out here, anyway? I bet you could find something closer to UT."

Sarah decided Hester was definitely making fun of her. "I need a job," she said. "I can't find anything else."

This was a lie. There were plenty of places near campus looking for summer help. But Turner, her boyfriend, didn't want to live near campus. They had moved out of their dorm that year, their first year of college, into an apartment on the last bus top from the University, in a scrap of neighborhood between the airport and a creek.

Their plan had been that Sarah would paint, and Turner would write. Turner, who lived off checks from his mother, offered to pay Sarah's tuition and rent. But Sarah had told him she didn't want to live that way.

Hester grinned crookedly, wrinkling her nose, as if she could smell Sarah's lie; she told Sarah she could have the job, if she wanted it.

That first month at the Pizza Hut, she made almost nothing. With tips, on her $2.13 minimum wage, she cleared $3.26 an hour. She'd lost her work-study scholarship at the fine arts library because of her dismal GPA. She didn't even know if she could afford to go back to UT in the fall. She needed to get on the dinner shift, to save to pay her tuition, which with fees would be over $600. Hester, in exchange for opening and closing, worked both the lunch and dinner rushes, driving home to Pflugerville in between to nap and feed her daughter, a deal she'd cut with the manager, a pale, moon-faced man named Mike, who flitted in and out of the restaurant like a ghost. Sarah didn't expect a deal like Hester's; she just needed a break.

After they cleaned up the lunch rush, wiping down tables, re-filling the salt, pepper, and sugar shakers, vacuuming the meaty residue off the floor, she and Hester went outside and smoked. Hester smoked, unapologetically—there was a little edge to her, Sarah thought, a crookedness and arrogance Sarah trusted. While they smoked, Hester savaged the lunch crowd—she was a talented mimic, especially of the moms—but Sarah wondered if this was just another performance, like her performance for the customers. It was always hard to tell what people really meant.

"You're not ready," Hester said, before Sarah even finished asking about the dinner shift. Hester stood, as always, left arm hooked across her waist, right arm levered over it, palm up; she flicked at her cigarette, gazing out across the empty parking lot as if at some distant country she would command.

Sarah wanted to ask Hester what in the fuck she had to do to be ready. She had been there since seven that morning, kneading dough, chopping vegetables, setting up the salad bar, rolling silverware, stacking plastic cups, filling various shakers, always a step behind Hester. For the last two hours, during the lunch rush, she had shuttled back and forth between the kitchen, the tables, the silverware station, the soda machines, countless times, like a lab rat in the experiment of capitalism. In high school, she'd worked shit jobs—slinging ice cream for a guy who stood behind her and pressed his hard-on into the small of her back, cleaning popcorn and sticky puddles off the floor of a movie theater run by meth heads—but she'd never had to work this hard. She felt dizzy with exhaustion. Hester told her she'd had a good day.

"You're too slow, for one thing," Hester said, answering the question Sarah hadn't asked. "Don't run the orders out fast enough, don't wipe the tables down fast enough, don't set them up fast enough, either. Dinner, everything's twice as fast.

"But it ain't just that," Hester added, as Sarah writhed with resentment, a kettle of snakes in her chest. "It's your attitude. You act all pretty, but customers can tell what you think of them. They can tell you don't really want to be here."

It was true. She didn't want to be there. Her first attempts at currying tips, aping Hester, hadn't worked. They were too flirty or too unctuous; the customers, sensing her insincerity, retreated from her with suspicion, even loathing. She had to create a version of herself, she knew, that was plausible enough for she herself to believe in. What she had thought worked best was a plainspoken, no-nonsense approach. She was not thrilled to be there, her Waitress Persona said. She would not be your best friend; she would not go behind the Dumpster and suck you off; but she would accurately and promptly fill your order. Even this persona required enormous artifice and self-control to maintain. She wondered if it were so difficult for Hester. She hated them: the pettifogging, dictatorial moms, the ravenous boys in stinking little league uniforms, the leering men, swilling beer, who slapped her ass, all of them eating, eating, eating, like pigs at a trough. Sometimes she imagined the robbers reappearing, calmly going about their business—not hurting anyone, just scaring the soccer moms and piggish men shitless.

"Do you want to be here?" she said.

Hester narrowed her eyes through her smoke, calculating, Sarah thought, how much she ought to be insulted. "Wanting ain't got nothing to do with it," Hester said. "This is where I am. You got to be where you are to get anyplace else."

Sarah wanted to ask Hester from what inspirational poster in the tiny manager's office she had gleaned such wisdom, but turned to ash her cigarette, so that Hester wouldn't see what she thought.

"What's your five-year plan?" Hester said, in a tone that suggested she'd seen Sarah's thought clearly. "Everybody needs a plan."

Had any friend of hers asked this question, Sarah would have considered it a joke. Sarah's friends didn't ask such things. But Hester wasn't joking. It reminded Sarah of questions her mother asked: What was she really going to do with her life? Meaning, what was she going to do that was not painting? Sarah didn't know how to answer without irony; and so, as she often did with Hester, she felt belittled, exposed.

"I'll tell you mine," Hester said. "I want to be Mike. I want to own one of these stores. That's where the real money is. You get yourself one of these, people work for you, you sit on your ass and make money. I don't even want to tell you how much this place pulls in, even on slow days. I cash out every night and carry the pouches over to the bank every morning. I know. You set yourself up in one of these, get it going right, borrow money from the bank to buy another one, then another. That's the really real money. That's Mike.

"Maybe, if you step up your game," Hester added, "I'll take you with me."

Sarah grimaced politely, not meeting Hester's eyes. She knew what Turner would say: That Hester was brutal and vulgar. That she sought to exploit others as she herself had been exploited. They had marked the clock tower at UT with red paint handprints to protest the University's investment in South Africa. Turner opposed private property of any kind. When they moved to the apartment, he said they were moving into the world of Gritty Realism. But this, what Hester believed in, Sarah thought, was the real world. The really real world. It was what Sarah's mother had to do after Sarah's father had left—start a cake decorating business, because she'd had nothing, not a house, not a job, certainly not a college degree.

"What about you?" Hester prodded.

What about her? Sarah thought. Her plan had been to get a scholarship at Cooper Union, but she'd choked, hadn't even applied. In high school, she'd won a statewide painting scholarship, then a tri-state, for her self-portraits. But now she was frozen, terrified. At UT, she'd taken gut requirements and one life drawing class, in which she had finished exactly one drawing, a reclining woman, her face caught in a rictus of pain. Sarah hated it—it looked like a female *pietà*, or the cover of a Joy Division album—melodramatic, pretentious, self-pitying.

She couldn't explain any of this to Hester. Hester would not go to college, then or ever; she would not win a scholarship of any kind. But neither, Sarah thought, could she explain herself right now to the art kids from her high school arts magnet, or the scrubbed and polished sorority girls in her life drawing class. She couldn't even explain where she was to Turner—or, worse, she had tried, and he hadn't understood, and worse, when he was drunk enough, he'd used what Sarah had told him to mock her.

"I don't know," she said.

"What about your boyfriend?"

"What about him?" Sarah said—unnerved, for a moment, that Hester had somehow read her mind.

"What's his plan?" Hester asked.

What was Turner's plan? Most days, when he wasn't sitting on the back porch, drinking gin, reading, he sat at his desk and wrote. Sarah didn't know what to think of this—whether to regard it, as her mother would, as obscenely self-indulgent, or with something like envy, like she had when she'd first met Turner, when she'd wished that she could be him.

She told Hester that Turner was a writer. Hester asked if he had a job; Sarah said that he wrote. Hester wrinkled her nose. She asked if Turner gave Sarah flowers, cooked her dinner, bought her nice things. Sometimes he cooked dinner, Sarah said.

"What are you with him for if he don't treat you right?" Hester said. "You're too smart and too pretty just to settle."

She thought that Hester must be joking, trying to bond with her, girl to girl, by complaining about men. She felt herself freeze up, as if Hester had touched her some place she shouldn't have. How could Hester fathom her relationship with Turner—how deeply entwined they were, how deeply in love? Anything she said in defense of Turner, Hester wouldn't understand, and anything she said in agreement with Hester would be a betrayal of Turner, and herself.

"At least tell me it's good sex," Hester said, actually prodding her elbow. "At least tell me he eats you out and don't just stick it in."

Sarah felt herself blush to the roots of her hair. All of her sex with Turner, like all her sex before him, with the skate punks and club boys from the Theater Gallery, and even boys she'd loved, or thought she'd loved, had occurred when she was drunk. When they first moved in, Turner and she had tried to do it sober, but it hadn't worked. The memory of them sitting on their mattress, avoiding each other's eyes like strangers on a bus, still made her cringe.

"It's great," she said, enraged. "We fuck like rabbits. How about you? Have you got a boyfriend?"

"I got a ex," Hester said, eyeing her. "We don't talk about him."

"Did he treat you right?" Sarah said, not caring, at that moment, if she got fired—nothing was worth it, she thought, this humiliation.

"We don't talk about him," Hester said, flicking her cigarette into the parking lot, swinging open the brown metal service door, all in one swift motion. Shouted Spanish and a blast of yeasty heat spilled out. Hester looked back over her shoulder, narrowing her blue-tinted eyes. Sarah braced herself to be fired.

"That don't matter," Hester said. "Men don't matter. I'm putting you on the dinner shift. I want you back here by five."

Walking home—it was still exciting to think of the apartment where they lived, as home—Sarah imagined what Turner would say when she told him she'd gotten the dinner shift. He would say she should be painting, instead of wasting her time at a McJob. She didn't know how to answer him without a fight. Why couldn't he be glad, she thought, just a little, for her crappy job, in which she'd discovered—she could barely admit it to herself, much less him—a little pride?

At the Goodwill, in the reassuring air-conditioned smell of old shoes, she found a blue bottle. The bottle would fit on the window ledge above the kitchen sink, where it would catch the afternoon light, or on the curio shelf in the dining room, where they had yet to put a table. On a rotating wire rack, she found a postcard of a cowboy leaping across a canyon: *The great leap of faith*, she wrote. *I am so in love with you and our life and our house.*

Outside again, in the terrific heat, she was still too far away, at the tattered apartment complex, where children darted, shouts and laughter and arguments threading through stairwells, tinny transistor hair metal and oompah of *norteño* polka drifting through open windows, to hear Turner's music. If she heard, through the windows of their apartment, *Blue* or *Astral Weeks*, he would be okay; but if it was Lightning Hopkins or *Exile on Main Street,* she braced herself for what version of him she would find. When she'd asked Turner if he wanted to live with her, he'd told her he couldn't live without her. She had already used her savings from her work-study for half the deposit and first month's rent. She couldn't go back to her mother's house; she didn't want to go back. Listening, she felt her gut tighten; she knew she had no place else to go.

At the clapboard duplex, she heard silence—she had learned to interpret this, too. She opened the front door, tried to jimmy it closed behind her, jiggling it back into its frame, then gave up, and slammed it shut. She climbed the stairs, footsore, exhausted; she didn't know how she would summon the energy for another shift.

Leaf-shadows shifted across bare wooden floors; the living room was empty except for her drawing of the reclining woman, two white metal lawn chairs, shelves made of cinderblock and four by eight planks that held their records and Turner's stereo; the dining room, empty except for knick-knacks on the curio shelf, and matchbox cars, marbles, bits of old machines she'd found in the creek behind the house; the back door in the kitchen, open to the empty porch. The apartment was like a movie set, she thought; she didn't want to paint it—she wanted to film it.

In their room, Turner sat at his desk in a white metal lawn chair, hunched over a yellow legal pad, his back to her, facing a window that looked out at the creek. Their mattress was free of its usual welter of ashtrays, magazines, and dirty clothes. The floor, too, was cleared, as were the floors in the living room and dining room and kitchen. She knew he had spent the morning cleaning. The spotless apartment, like his rigid, hunched figure, was a rebuke; if she could work, if she could contribute, he could, too.

She stood behind him, waiting for him to turn to her; she knew he had heard her slam the front door. The desk

113

was bare except for a neat pile of yellow paper anchored by a rock. He was dressed, as usual, in khaki pants and a long-sleeved button-down shirt, clothes that even in the house's relative coolness must have been stiflingly hot. In the dorm, they'd spent days around each other naked—drinking, reading, fucking, talking about Art—but here, in the apartment, they had disappeared.

She waited, shifting her weight from one foot to another; he bent closer to his work. She imagined hurling the bottle through the window, then set it carefully on the floor. She wanted very badly to take a shower, then a nap; but first, she wanted him to turn to her.

"Hey," she said. "I brought you something."

He hooked his arm over the back of his chair. His eyes were hard and injured-looking, his face spiteful and pale; but still, she felt a foolish flutter at the pit of her stomach, looking at him. She handed him the bag, keeping her distance. He fished out the card, then the bottle, then glanced up at her, his eyes glassy with tears; she wondered if he'd already started in on the bottle he kept under the sink. If he would only get up and show a little tenderness, she thought, it might be better—not perfect, but better.

He set the blue bottle on the desk, where it caught the afternoon light, just as she'd imagined. "Thank you," he said. "It's beautiful."

"I have to work tonight," she said.

He turned back to the window. "What about the porch?"

Each night, they sat on the porch, drinking and arguing about whether she should quit her job. They argued, she thought, so that they could make up, when

114

they were drunk. For Turner, it was a kind of foreplay, but she hated it.

Some nights, he read from the novel he was writing. In it, a character like the boy next door, whom they had watched coming and going from the creek, returned to discover that both of his parents had vanished, then his grandparents, then his teachers. Later, she would try to remember if it had been any good. She couldn't imagine that it was; but at the time, she had tried to believe it was good.

"I'm sorry," she said. "I have to work."

"You don't have to," he said.

"Yes, I do, Turner. I need the money."

Not like him, she didn't say; and he didn't say that they could use the money his mother sent him. "I need the money," she said. "And Hester asked me."

"Hester?" he said. "The one with the big hair and the baby?"

"Yes, Hester," she said, regretting how she'd described Hester to Turner.

She sat on the mattress and stripped off the black nylon stockings the Pizza Hut Corporation required her to wear, which were damp with grease and sweat. All she wanted was to rest, but she could feel him revving himself up for a fight.

"You don't have to," he said, eyeing her bare legs.

"Yes, Turner, I do. I really do. I'll make it up later. We can sit on the porch and do whatever, talk about whatever. But I have to go to work."

He looked out the window again, stung, she thought, by her words.

"You don't have to," he said. "You're choosing to. You're running away from yourself. You're an artist, and you're running away from yourself."

"Jesus Christ, Turner."

"It's true," he said. "This is how it happens. The death of the heart."

Her high school art teacher, Mr. Monson, who had entered her self-portraits in the scholarship competitions, had called her this—an Artist. She knew that Turner held an image of her, some cross between Patti Smith and Freda Kahlo—The Art Punk Girl, who was tough and brilliant and took no shit, an image she'd created.

Sometimes, when she was buzzed enough, or exhausted enough from whatever shitty job, she could imagine herself as someone different. Turner called it the Bullshit Channel. But it wasn't bullshit; it was survival. It was the Waitress Persona; it was the Good Student. It wasn't Bulimic Girl, puffy-faced, raccoon-eyed; it wasn't the Skank who fucked skinheads in the Theater Gallery bathroom; it wasn't the Fuckup who came to school drunk. The drinking or purging or fucking were all routes to a sadness and self-disgust somehow final and magnificent, transcendent. The only place she could turn it into something else, something different from herself, was when she painted. Which was why she hadn't painted since she'd come to college. If she went to that place—that place she could ride all night, drinking wine, smoking cigarettes in her room at her mother's house—she could almost grasp it—the ache of nothingness, the staring human masks, the world's vast oceanic intricateness—and paint it—she believed that there would be nothing left of her, Sarah, whoever that might be.

"It's just a job, Turner," she said.

"I'll pick you up," he said to the window.

"You don't have to."

"I have to. It's not safe, your walking home in this neighborhood."

"What are you going to do while I'm at work?"

"I don't know," he said, stiffening. "Maybe I'll keep writing."

"Turner," she said, touching his shirt, which was warm and damp with his sweat. "This is important to me."

He flinched, shrinking from her, pretending to scrutinize the page before him. "Don't worry," he said. "I won't embarrass you."

Later, she would think, she could have told him that Hester would give her a ride home, and he would have quietly passed out. Maybe then, she would have gotten to bed earlier, and to the Pizza Hut the next morning on time. Maybe then, she would have stopped what happened to Hester.

Hester was right. Everything was faster. The parties were bigger, the orders were more complex; but Sarah wouldn't let herself be defeated. She would not betray the confidence Hester had shown in her. She would not let herself be defeated by her own exhaustion, or the quivering ache in her arms and shoulders from carrying the trays laden with pizza and pasta; she'd napped on the mattress while Turner wrote, and dreamt they were back in the dorm, painting watercolors, talking about Roland Barthes and the indeterminacy of the signifier, whatever that was—and everything was beautiful, everything was as it had been. When she woke up, Turner had already gone to the back porch with a jar of gin and ice and *The Drama of the Gifted Child* on his lap, and didn't answer her when she said goodbye; but she would not let this defeat her, either, her worry about what she would face that night. She didn't worry about whether the Waitress Persona was true, or not. This was her first night on the dinner shift, her Waitress Persona told her customers, and they were working together to keep her job; and it was not a lie.

By the time Hester turned the lock on the plate glass doors and began to run the register, Sarah thought that she had changed, if only because she had pushed past a limit of exhaustion into some new realm of fatigue she had not thought possible, as if she had shed one skin for another. She kept going, jacked up on Diet Coke from a huge plastic cup she'd parked next to the drink machine, clearing the buffet of pizza dried under the heat lamps to the stiffness of shoe leather, carrying trays crowded with clear plastic wells of salad makings from the salad bar, wrapping them, putting them in the walk-in cooler if they were still fresh, dumping them if they weren't, shuttling trays of plates, cups, and silverware to the dishwashers, wiping down the tables, running the vacuum. In her apron, as she ran through her tasks, seventy, maybe eighty dollars in tips tapped against her waist—a reassuring weight, a weight that was also lightness, freedom.

Hester checked off the credit card receipts. Dark crescents shadowed her blue eyes; her hair was lank with sweat and grease. Sarah wished she could get a box of crayons, a kid's paper menu, and sketch her. During the dinner rush, she had filled in drinks and silverware on Sarah's tables, and Sarah had done the same, a delicate, complex dance. Now, even the dishwashers had left, the machines silenced; the empty restaurant, the taillights passing on the freeway outside, seemed theirs.

"You did pretty good," Hester said.

Sarah didn't know what to say—she wanted to tell Hester she was glad she'd made her proud; but she knew that would be foolish—Hester was her boss, not her mother, not her friend.

Someone banged outside on the plate glass door. Hester reached for the phone next to the register, then stopped, frozen in place, watching Sarah where she stood near the kitchen. A bolt of fear shot through Sarah, too, the fear that Hester must have felt, Sarah thought, when the robbers came; and she was ashamed she hadn't tried to imagine what Hester had felt, until then.

"It's just Turner," she said.

Hester stood at the register, her hand still hovering above the phone.

Outside, Turner swayed, silhouetted by streetlight—loose, looming, a flag in the dark. He waved, ghostly, grinning his crooked grin. Sarah waved back—yet still she hesitated, wondering what would happen if she didn't open the door. But of course she had to open the door. Of course she had to let him in.

He sidled past her, pecking her cheek, breathing the astringent odor of gin. He wore khaki slacks and a button-down shirt, as if he had arrived for a prep school date.

As always, when he was drunk, he seemed to take up too much room. He waved at Hester, grinning, his eyes narrowed with fixed drunken certainty, as if the Pizza Hut and her job and Hester were all some ironic joke.

"So this is where the magic happens," he said to the empty tables. "You're Circe," he said to Hester. "You're the magician."

She was ashamed of him, she thought, as clearly as if someone had spoken the words—then, instantly, ashamed of herself; she hoped his act was all just a joke, just a lark, that in a blink of the eye, might vanish.

Hester watched Turner closely, her hand on the phone. "I'll close up," she said. "You go on home."

"I want to help," Sarah said.

"He can't be in here," said Hester; then, to Turner, "You're drunk—you know that, right? You're drunk, and you're underage. Which is illegal. I could lose my liquor license. So I'm going to need you to leave."

Turner raised his hands in mock surrender. "I'm fine," he said. "I can help."

"He'll be quiet," Sarah said.

"Yes, I'll be quiet. I am very good at being quiet. It's essential for poets. Negative capability. The agenbite of inwit."

"Are y'all not hearing me?" Hester said. "Get him out, or I call the cops."

Turner swayed, staring, a stiff smile plastered on his face. For a moment, Sarah almost felt sorry for him.

"Who do you think you are?" he said to Hester.

Sarah touched his arm.

"She's told me all about you," he said. "About your

baby and your mother. About how you have to drive all the way from Pflugerville."

"Turner," Sarah said.

He batted away her hand. She closed her other hand over the fingers he'd struck, not so much from pain, but shock. He had never hit her before. But when Hester lifted the phone, Sarah shook her head, once; it would only make things worse.

"Do you know who she is?" Turner said. "She's an artist. She's won prizes for her painting. I bet you didn't know that, did you?

"Did you?" he said.

"No, I didn't," Hester said to Sarah.

"I didn't think so," Turner said.

"I know she's a good worker," Hester said, calmly—to show, Sarah knew, that she wasn't afraid of him.

"I know something else," Hester continued. "Cause we talk, you know, woman to woman, and I know things. Women things."

"Sure." Turner guffawed stagily—afraid, Sarah thought, of what Hester would say. "Women things," he said.

"I can tell when a woman ain't happy," Hester said. "She ain't happy. One day she's going to figure that out and move on. So why don't you just save yourself the trouble and move on first?"

Turner squinted at Hester, then at Sarah; Sarah knew he thought she'd told Hester that she wanted to leave.

"Come on," he said to Sarah.

"You don't need to do that," Hester said. "You can stay right here."

Turner grasped her arm, digging in his fingers.

"Let's go," he said.

Hester lifted the phone again. "You best release her," she said. "I got no problem calling the cops. You won't like what they'll do to you."

Turner hesitated, then let go, glaring at Hester.

"I'm sorry," Sarah said. "I'll come back in the morning."

"You can stay here," Hester said, watching Sarah as she had that afternoon, when she'd told Sarah to come back for the dinner shift—with what Sarah saw, now, was pity.

Her hand still smarted. She could still feel Turner's fingers clutching her arm. Turner stalked ahead of her across the parking lot between the cars that were always there, in which, Sarah now saw, from the faint lights in them, people lived. When they had met in the dorm, she had shown him pictures of her self-portraits, and they had talked about William Burroughs and Lydia Lunch, Joseph Cornell and Richard Diebenkorn. His hands, on her, had been gentle. Now she was afraid to go back with him to the dark, empty apartment.

Around the corner from the liquor store, the ragged apartment complexes pumped out *bachata* and top forty. The parking lot in front of the Carousel Lounge was filled with hulking cars, its windowless plywood front painted with crude circus scenes of acrobats with blunted limbs.

"Turner?" she said. "Let's get a drink."

He stopped in the street, grinning at her—thinking,

she saw, that he had won. She despised his arrogance, how he had insulted Hester, and humiliated her. But she needed time, she told herself, to think about what she would do.

In the Carousel Lounge, men in polyester suits and clean blue jeans and women in flowered dresses milled, shuffling around a broken parquet dance floor. At the wobbly table where Sarah sat, an ashtray overflowed onto an oilcloth the color of dried blood. She lit a cigarette, glad to be off her feet. Soon, Turner would come back with drinks paid for out of her tip money. When they first moved to the apartment, they had come to watch the couples dance, and she had felt a sadness sweet and seemingly profound, a nostalgia for what she hadn't yet lived. The men led the women gently, decorously, she'd thought; the women looked up at them, trusting them. Now she saw in the women's uplifted gazes only desperation and fatigue; she felt ashamed, being there, watching them—her mother would have fit right in.

Her mother had grown up on a farm in Western Minnesota, a place so remote and obscure that she hadn't seen a telephone inside a house until she was nineteen, Sarah's age. She had met Sarah's father at a barn dance. Her father, whose day job had been electrical engineering, was an artist—or at least, he called himself one. At night, in their basement in Dallas, he drew boxes. For years, he showed them only to Sarah—impossible boxes, spheroids and tetrahedrons, structures that folded in on themselves in impossible dimensions—until he himself had disappeared. She hadn't seen him since she'd started high school. She didn't know if he was alive.

Of course, she had told Turner all of this, when he had

still been Turner, when they had talked about such things.

Turner put their drinks on the table, then sat, wobbling the table, averting his eyes from her. She wondered if he felt anything that she did—sadness, or shame—himself.

The first warm glow of booze hit, a burst of light at the back of her skull. She pictured Hester in the Pizza Hut, running down the checklist before she left: locking the cash and receipts in the safe, cleaning the bathrooms, turning off the lights. There was still time, she told herself, to go back.

"Turner?" she said. "You shouldn't have said all that."

He twisted away from her in his chair, sloshing the drinks, crossing one khakied leg over the other. "Turner?" she said. "Are you listening to me?"

"I am listening," he said.

"You shouldn't have said all that. You shouldn't have done that. You shouldn't have hit me and grabbed me."

He nodded, not facing her. "Was it true, what she said?"

"Was what true?" she said, knowing what he meant.

"That you want to leave," he said.

"I don't know, Turner. If it's like this, I can't stay."

"It wouldn't be like this if you were painting," he said, watching the dancers. "I've told you. I'll give you the money."

"I can't do that. I have to do it on my own."

"You aren't really doing anything, though, are you? Except wallowing in your own shit. Are you?" He glanced at her, grinning, ghastly with spite and self-hate. "You won't leave. We're meant to be together. You can't."

He turned back to the dancers, disappearing as quickly

as he had come.

"Do you want another drink?" he said.

She knew she should get up, go back to the Pizza Hut, try to catch Hester before she left. But she waited, watching for some other Turner, the Turner she had known, to appear, the humid stink of cigarettes and first leaden wave of booze settling on her like a blanket.

"Sure," she said.

Then she was drunk, drunker than she had thought. Then they were in the dark apartment, kissing each other hungrily, fumbling off clothes, as if one or the other of them might vanish.

Maybe, she thought later, if she hadn't gone to the Carousel Lounge that night, if she had gotten up early the next morning, the robbers wouldn't have returned, seeing two girls at the Pizza Hut, instead of one. Maybe, even if they had come, she could have saved Hester from being beaten when they robbed her. Maybe she, not Hester, would have been beaten—so badly, *The Daily Texan* reported, that Hester, an unidentified employee, was taken to the St. David's ICU. Sarah thought of Aanya, then—whether she would be brought to see Hester, whether Hester would even survive. Then she chided herself for her trashy fantasizing, just the flip side of the treacly hope that kept her with Turner. She knew what Hester would think of her fantasies—that they were mawkish, sentimental, childish.

It took her until the next summer to go back to the Pizza Hut. By then, she had broken up with Turner, begged back a job at the fine arts library, bought a Super 8 camera, started making short movies. The Pizza Hut was the same—the same yeasty smell, another blond girl taking orders at the tables. No one knew who Sarah was, except Mike, who laid into her for not coming to work the morning it was robbed. She was irresponsible, he said. Hester had lost her sight in one eye. But there was a silver lining, he said: Hester now managed his San Marcos store. As if, Sarah thought, this was compensation. Then she upbraided herself. She'd imagined what Hester had felt—the fists pummeling her, the terror of not knowing when it would stop—though she knew it was nothing like what Hester had actually felt. Her life, she knew, was still theoretical; one direction seemed just as possible, just as true, as any other. But she knew that this had never been true for Hester.

The night that she and Turner went to the Carousel Lounge, none of this had happened—though when she remembered it, it seemed as if everything had already happened, as if it didn't really need to happen to be true. Turner was fucking her, not gently, as he had at the dorm, looking down at her, his face silvered with streetlight. The blue bottle cast a streak of blue shadow across the ceiling. She wondered what Hester would see, if she could see her—Turner sticking it in. She looked away, ashamed of what she saw, as if she were watching herself in a movie; and she felt herself turn smooth, adamantine, impenetrable. Don't argue with them, she thought. Don't look them in the eye. Just give them the money.

Pictures of the Shark

On the freeway, the tires of his father's car made heartbeats, like the music in *Jaws* that signaled the great shark's approach. Everywhere Buddy went, the shark followed— grinning, deadly, a silent friend.

Buddy sat in the back seat, wedged next to suitcases his father had lugged out of the woman's apartment; the woman sat in front, in Buddy's place. All the way from Houston through Dallas, her thin, breathless voice had fluttered over road signs and billboards, license plates and historical markers, circling what a good time they were going to have together on their trip to Universal Studios, in Hollywood.

"It's so nice that we can all finally be together," she said. "I think we're going to be special friends, Buddy. Don't you?"

The woman paused, waiting for an answer. Buddy

pressed his forehead against his window. Outside, a freight train seemed to move slowly backward. At night, trains moaned past the house where Buddy and his mother lived, where his father used to live; Buddy wondered if any of the cars he saw would pass his mother's house. He closed one eye and framed the picture he would take, like leaving a note in a bottle. His mother's camera was a thin black plastic rectangle whose lens was grimed with sand from trips to the beach with his father long ago. Buddy hadn't told his father that he had his mother's camera. The night before, he'd slipped it into his suitcase so he could get pictures of Bruce, the mechanical shark from *Jaws,* at Universal. His mother had caught him and said it would've been okay for him to bring it, if he'd asked; now, she'd said, he'd have to take some pictures for her.

"Buddy?" his father said. "Answer Mary."

In the rearview mirror, his father's eyes floated, watching him. That morning, Buddy had followed him down a long hallway at an apartment complex that looked like a set in a disaster movie, ready at any moment to be destroyed. His father had knocked on a door, then opened it impatiently. Inside, the woman, who stood barely taller than Buddy, backed away. Buddy could not help compare her pale, sleek arms to his mother's, which were plump and jiggly. Ashamed, he looked at the woman's face. She studied him anxiously with timid, slate-colored eyes. To Buddy, it was clear she was a liar. Even before he'd met her, he'd known she was, and his mother had told him a liar was the worst thing in the world.

"Buddy," his father said. "If you don't answer Mary, we're gonna pull over."

"Yes, ma'am," Buddy said to his window. "I'd like that."

The woman, whose name was Mary Winifreed, didn't reply. Buddy had known his father had a secret, but still he'd come. So what did that make him? One thing was sure: He couldn't let his mother know. He didn't want a picture of Mary Winifreed.

In his mother's photo album, a fading world of trips and birthday parties, Buddy's father played horseback with him, and walked with him on the beach, and taught him how to fix a car. Three summers before, when the last pictures in the album were taken, his father had left to finish medical school and serve out his time in the Army. When he called home, he told Buddy about autopsies he'd done on soldiers who'd shot each other while training, or drowned in a lake. Listening to him, Buddy had felt frightened and adult. When his father returned at the beginning of the summer, his eyes were hooded and strange, and he'd told Buddy to call him "sir." He said he lived with his own mother, Buddy's grandmother. Even on weekends, he wore two-piece suits and smelled of Bay Rum and Listerine and moved with a robot's herky-jerky gait. Sometimes, he visited Buddy's house late at night; Buddy lay awake, listening to sounds from his mother's room that were like crying, though he knew that was not what they were.

But each Saturday, Buddy's father took him to the movies. His father preferred outlaw movies, which gave Buddy nightmares, but he didn't complain. In the theaters' cool darkness, he stole glances at his father's long, handsome, hurt-looking face.

Last month, when they'd seen *Star Wars*, his father had leaned over to him and said, as he always did, "Back in a minute. Tell me what happens while I'm gone."

A moment later, heart hammering, Buddy snuck after him into a dim hallway. His father leaned over a pay phone, his gray suit rumpled like a spy's.

"Should be done by six-thirty," he said, in a voice Buddy had never heard him use before; it was slow and patient, as if he were talking to a child. "Then I have to take him to his mother's. I know you want to see him, honey, but you can't, okay? She might sue me, then I'll never see him again."

His father hung up and pulled his hand down his face, as if pulling off a mask. Buddy retreated. In the theater, he tried to find the row where they had sat, then gave up and picked one. His chest felt weighted with the mystery of his father's life, and his heart beat heavily with hope and fear.

After the movie, while his father drove, Buddy explained that the space ships in *Star Wars* were actually models filmed in front of matte screens. If his father had looked closely, he would have noticed, at their edges, a blue glimmer.

The special effects in *Jaws*, Buddy reminded him, were better. While his father had been in the Army, Buddy had persuaded his mother to take him to see it fifteen times, and though he had read about the workings of the shark, they remained mysterious to him. Now, he recounted the crew's heroic efforts to keep Bruce from running amok;

sometimes, he had attacked them as if he were real.

"Maybe we'll visit him," his father said, looking sideways at him, as he had since he'd found Buddy in the theater. "How'd you like that?"

If he said yes, Buddy knew, he would have to keep his father's secret. "Yes, sir," he said. "I'd like that."

When they walked up the broken cement path to their house, his mother watched them, her face blurred and ghostly behind a porch screen. As always when his father appeared, she stood very still, as if afraid to startle him. His father stopped, one foot on the bottom step. His mother asked if he could come in. Just for a minute. Just for a minute, his father said. His mother held the screen door open, and when his father angled past her, she stood on her toes and kissed him. Buddy tried to slip past behind them, but his mother caught his arm. Here we are, she said.

She looked down at Buddy, her eyes sharp and fierce, already seeing the secret he carried. His father's eyes were watery and pink. Be good to your mother, he said. Buddy told him he would, then hurried to his darkening room. His parents' voices rumbled through the wall behind his bed. That would be great, his mother said. We could all go. It's not like that, his father said. It's not that way anymore.

Then what way is it? his mother had said.

The motel room was small and dimly lit. Two beds with red woolen blankets faced a bureau, on top of which sat a battered TV. While they unloaded the car, Mary Winifreed kept touching Buddy— light taps on his back, tiny hands on his shoulder. His father glanced at them, frowning. After they finished with the car, he announced it was time for Buddy to call his mother. "Give us a minute," he said to Mary Winifreed.

Mary Winifreed retreated to the bathroom, her mouth a tight line. His father rolled his eyes, as he did sometimes when Buddy's mother got upset. When they'd left Houston, he had promised his mother that Buddy would call every night.

His father sat on a bed and waved Buddy over to the one across from him. He picked up the receiver, then cupped his hand over its mouthpiece.

"Your mother's a wonderful woman," he said.

Buddy nodded. "Yes, sir."

"We don't want to do anything to hurt her, do we?"

"No, sir."

"You're a smart kid," his father said. "You understand a lot more than I did when I was your age. You know a lot about the movies."

Blushing, Buddy stared down at his hands, which were clenched and dirty.

"Look at me," his father said, lowering his voice. "I'm real proud of you. I wanted to take you on this trip so we can get to know each other better, and so you can get to know Mary Winifreed. But you understand it would hurt your mother real badly if she knew Mary was here, don't you? I don't need to explain that to you, do I?"

"No, sir."

His father smiled as if he were in pain. "Good," he said.

"Yes, sir," Buddy said.

"You don't have to call me that here," his father said. "Call me 'dad.'"

Buddy looked at the dingy, swimming pool-colored walls, and the dead green eye of the TV, and then at his father. "Okay, dad," he said.

After his father spoke to an operator, he handed Buddy the phone. Buddy saw his mother in their bright yellow kitchen, a box of orange snack crackers and a glass of wine on the table next to her. Though he was ten years old, sometimes he still sat on her lap, burying his face in her white uniform, breathing the smell of the laboratory where she worked.

"Honey," she said. "Is that you?"

"Yes, momma," he said.

"Are you okay? You don't sound like yourself."

Buddy felt dizzy and sick, as if he were on top of a tall building, itching to jump. "Yes, momma," he said. "I'm fine."

His father took the phone and said Buddy needed to go to the bathroom. Yes, he said, Buddy was fine; he looked at Buddy and Buddy looked away. What do you mean? his father asked. Of course he sounds fine. Buddy took off his shoes and got under the covers; it seemed wrong to take off his clothes. He shut his eyes. His father's voice, so weary and adult that Buddy could almost believe what it said was true, told his mother a version of their day in which only he and Buddy appeared. Tomorrow, he said, they'd try to make it to his parents' cabin in Colorado. Yes, he said, he would be careful. Now, they needed to get some sleep.

Then there was silence, in which Buddy knew his mother told his father that she loved him. His father gently replaced the phone in its cradle. Springs creaked as his father rose from the bed, and gunshots and the trample of hooves filtered from the TV. Buddy kept his eyes closed. The bathroom door creaked open.

"Does she want you to call her every night?" Mary Winifreed asked.

His father said he didn't know. "I don't call that helping," he said to Buddy. "If you were in the Army, they'd march your ass in the heat 'till you dropped."

Buddy lay perfectly still.

"What's wrong, darling?" Mary Winifreed said.

His father's weight settled next to Buddy, and his rough, clean-smelling fingers tapped Buddy's nose. "What're you doin', playing possum?" he said, his voice quivering with anger. "Don't you know you can't lie to me?"

"Jimmy?" Mary Winifreed said. "What do you mean? Let him sleep."

By the time they reached Amarillo, Mary Winifreed had persuaded Buddy to stop calling her "ma'am," though he did not call her "Mary," either; he did not call her anything. This didn't prevent her from acting as if they were great friends. She promised him the use of her sewing scissors to clip ads for a special re-release of *Jaws*, which would assure its spot as top moneymaker of all time. He planned to collect the ads in a notebook in his suitcase.

When Mary Winifreed said that he must be very brave to have seen it so many times, and suggested they might see it together, he didn't answer her; he hadn't seen *Jaws* with his father, yet, and didn't want to with Mary Winifreed.

That morning, Buddy had woken to her rummaging in his suitcase. When she'd gone outside, he sprung from the bed, and found his clothes inside neatly folded. Before he could check on his mother's camera, he'd heard someone coming.

Now, he was afraid his father would discover the camera, and that Mary Winifreed already had.

But if they had, neither of them said anything. In Muleshoe, where the horizon was as flat and empty as a tabletop, Buddy popped the trunk, keeping an eye on his father, who stood with his back to him, pumping gas. Mary Winifreed had gone to the bathroom. Buddy dug out his notebook, then unzipped the side pocket, and felt inside. The camera was still there. "What'che got?" his father said.

"Nothing, dad," Buddy said, closing the trunk, wishing he'd been caught.

At his grandparents' cabin, Mary Winifreed exclaimed over the iron trivets and red-and-white checkered wallpaper and his grandmother's collection of glass telephone pole insulators, which trapped sunlight on the sill of a picture window like crystal balls. Long ago, Buddy and his parents and grandparents had come to the cabin on vacation. Buddy remembered firelight, and shimmying shadows, and his grandfather's voice telling tales of the Injun Chief, who scalped little boys while they slept, and of the Gray Ghost, who pickaxed whole families. When Buddy had cried and hidden his face in his mother's lap, his father and grandfather had laughed, telling him they were just stories.

"It feels like home," Mary Winifreed said, brushing her hand across the back of a chair, coming to rest near his father. "Why don't you get your camera? We could take some pictures for your parents."

His father stood in the doorway, goggling his eyes at Buddy. "Why do they need pictures?" he said. "They know what it looks like."

"Silly." Mary Winifreed touched his father's tie. "They'll want pictures of us."

Buddy wanted to slap Mary Winifreed, to tell her to stop ruining everything. But his father looked down at her and said, "Okay. Just a couple."

On tiptoe, anchoring herself with his tie, Mary Winifreed kissed his father. Buddy stared at the floor. He looked up. His father grimaced at him, but didn't move. Before he could stop himself, Buddy said, "I brought a camera."

Slowly, his father unhooked his arm from Mary Winifreed's shoulder.

"It's my mother's," Buddy said to Mary Winifreed.

"Look at me," Buddy's father said to him. "Did your mother tell you to bring it?"

"No, sir," Buddy said.

"Get it," his father said. "We'll be outside."

Buddy ran to the rear of the cabin. Behind him, in the living room, the screen door to the deck slammed. He unzipped his suitcase with trembling hands. The camera smelled of sand and seagrass and crabs. He remembered his father lifting him above the gray Gulf waves, the rise of water and taste of salt, his father's huge fingers encircling his ribcage.

He took the camera to the living room. Through the screen door, he saw Mary Winifreed and his father at the deck railing.

Across the valley, a jagged line of mountains swallowed the sun. Except for her pale sleek arms, Mary Winifreed was almost invisible. His father leaned close to her, speaking in the voice that Buddy had heard at the movies.

Buddy opened the screen door. His father turned and crossed the deck and took the camera, not looking at him. Mary Winifreed looked at him; her face was flushed and her eyes brimmed with tears. His father held the camera up to the fading light to read the number of the exposure, one; the roll was new.

"Does your mother know you have this?" he asked.

"Yes, sir," Buddy said.

"Did she ask you to take pictures?"

Buddy hesitated, unsure how to answer. "Yes, sir."

His father shook his head, a single sharp shudder of disgust. Mary Winifreed put her hand on his arm. "Jimmy? You told me it wouldn't be like this."

His father averted his face from her. "I want to talk to Buddy."

She tugged at his sleeve. "Why won't you let him? She already knows."

"Enough," his father said. "I need to talk to my son."

Mary Winifreed looked at Buddy, her mouth open; she let go of his father's arm and hurried into the cabin. A small cold flame of triumph flickered in Buddy, but was quickly dimmed by fear. In the twilight, his father's face swarmed with shadows.

"Sit down," his father said.

They sat at a worn picnic table. In the shadows, his father's face seemed broken, like a scattered jigsaw puzzle; his voice, when he spoke, was hollow. "I know you heard what Mary said, but she's wrong. If your mother finds out about her, Buddy, she'll pick me clean. You're the only one who can help. Not your mother. Not Mary Winifreed."

Buddy looked down at his hands, which were tightly folded, as though in prayer. His heart called out: *I will help! I will help!* But he kept silent, waiting.

"What if we told your mother you lost the camera?"

"No, sir," Buddy said, more loudly than he'd intended; he looked up at his father and lowered his voice. "Please, sir. Can we just take pictures of us?"

"Okay, Buddy," his father said, turning from him. "We'll try."

Later, Buddy lay in bed, listening to cicadas and a hoot owl. After his father dialed the operator and handed him the phone, Buddy had answered his mother's questions, tracing lines between red-and-white checks in an oilcloth on the dining room table. When she asked to talk to his father, Buddy looked up, and his father was gone. Buddy told his mother that his father was in the bathroom. After a long pause, she said, "Okay, honey. Tell him to call me when he can."

Now, Buddy pulled the cord of a lamp beside his bed, unzipped his suitcase, and opened its canvas pouch. In his notebook were his drawings of Bruce. Since his father had returned, on pieces of construction paper and his mother's lab reports and grocery bags, Buddy had drawn the shark, trying to get him right.

Now, as always, he began with the shark's conical snout, then his arching back. Then his dorsal fin, like a scimitar. His back tapered, though the muscles there, Buddy knew, were as powerful as pistons in a steam engine. The scythe of his tail propelled him forward. His medial fins balanced his flight through the water. Then his jaws. Row after row, his teeth folded out like petals in a flower. As he drew their serrated edges, their deadly tips, he bit the soft inside of his cheek until he tasted blood.

From his jeans pocket, Buddy took the piece of paper, worn smooth as a page from a Bible, on which his father had written instructions for calling his mother collect. He sat on his motel bed and stared at his reflection in a blank TV. Since they'd left Colorado, he'd had his own room. It was his first night in Hollywood.

Two nights had passed since he'd talked to his mother. The first night he called her, when they were at the Grand Canyon, he'd told her his father had gone for a walk. There was a long silence; then she started asking tricky questions, like whether Buddy had clean socks, and whether his father packed extra towels. After two more calls, Buddy had stopped, afraid to call her again, and afraid to tell his father he hadn't.

Though his father had never actually said so, Buddy understood that in order to get the camera back, and to take pictures of Bruce, he had to lie, though he never used this word anymore. At night, he swam in motel pools, sleek beneath the cool green water, silent even to himself.

The farther they got from Houston, the more his father talked. He expounded upon patterns of migrant labor and the history of the railroads, the construction of grain elevators and origins of the Great Salt Lake. In motel lobbies and all-night diners, he introduced Mary Winifreed as his wife, and she flushed with embarrassment and pleasure, glancing up as if to catch him in a joke.

Wherever they went, his father let Mary Winifreed take pictures with his mother's camera, though her picture could never be taken by it. Sometimes she offered to let Buddy use the camera, but his father wouldn't allow him to touch it. When she tried to talk to him alone, Buddy always found a way to mention his mother, which turned Mary Winifreed ashen and silent. Once, she'd said, "It's better, now that she knows. I'm sure she's a wonderful woman. I'd like to meet her some day." Buddy was tempted to tell her that his mother didn't know anything, and neither did she, but he knew it would be as sure a way to lose the camera as if he told his mother about Mary Winifreed. At the Grand Canyon, Buddy wished the wind would lift Mary Winifreed up and whisk her off; at the Hoover Dam, that she would slip into the still black water and be sucked into a turbine, or eaten by sharks. Faced with the cameras—his own and Buddy's mother's—his father leered and grimaced, and sometimes refused to let her take his picture at all.

Late at night, Buddy woke, swatting creatures from his feet. Through the wall behind his bed seeped Mary Winifreed's thin cries, and Buddy recognized them as the same ones he'd heard at his mother's house.

Now, as if at the end of a long tunnel, Buddy saw his

mother alone in the bright yellow kitchen. He picked up the receiver and dialed before he could think any more.

When the operator spoke, his mother asked, Where was he? Was he all right? Did he have any idea how worried she'd been? Did his father?

"Where is your father?" she said. "I want to talk to him."

If he knocked on the door that adjoined the rooms, a stray word might get caught in the line. "Daddy can't talk right now," he said. "He'll talk to you later."

"Don't give me that crap," his mother said, in a voice he'd only heard her use with his father; then she moaned softly. "Oh, honey," she said. "Please don't lie to me."

"I'm not lying," Buddy said. "You don't even know what's going on."

"Then tell me."

The humming line was a net that could kill him, a web that a word could shatter. "You can't make me," he said, before he hung up.

The next morning, Buddy ran toward the entrance of Universal Studios. Earlier, when he'd asked his father when he could use the camera, his father had said, "Soon," but so sharply Buddy was afraid to ask again. Already, he'd woken with a knot in his stomach; he was going to find out how Bruce really worked. Mary Winifreed had asked him if he was excited to see the shark. Buddy said he guessed so, then looked at her, wondering how much she knew about his agreement with his father. Now, he felt his stomach tighten with a cold and nameless fear. Ahead of him loomed the familiar image: a silver-blue shark rising like a missile, above which a naked woman struggled across the surface of the water; and beneath it, in red lettering: *JAWS*. As he came closer, he noticed it was stained with brown grime. In T*he Los Angeles Times,* he'd found a tiny ad for a two-week run at a dollar theater, dwarfed by a full-page spread declaring *Star Wars* the top moneymaker of all time.

Inside the park—UNIVERSAL STUDIOS FAMILY PARK, read the signs—Mary Winifreed was pressed against him in the crowd, fanning herself with a floppy straw hat, her gray eyes tired and watchful. His father loosened his tie, but seemed to vibrate a heat all his own. His smile was clenched, and his eyes darted, seeking an escape. Slung across his shoulder was a leather camera bag, which smelled of metal and oil. Buddy told himself he would ask again, soon.

Beyond the press of bodies, a guide's voice welcomed them to Universal Studios Family Park. In a little while, a whistle would direct them to the trolley. Until then, the guide said, they were free to buy souvenirs and refreshments in the Welcome Mall.

In the Welcome Mall, which was disguised by stucco walls and red-tiled roofs as a Spanish village, his father took a place in line at a hot dog stand, which spilled gouts of meaty steam into the leaden air. At a chest-high table protected from the baking sun by a miniature umbrella, they ate, sweating. The hot dogs were dry and gristly, but Buddy reminded himself that a shark could eat anything.

Soon, Buddy knew, Mary Winifreed would prevail

upon his father to take pictures. First, she would arrange him and his father with his arm around his father's waist, and his father's arm around his shoulder, like a father and son on TV. Then his father would take his camera, and Mary Winifreed would press her slim flank against Buddy's side. Before the shutter clicked, Buddy would cross his eyes, or stare at the ground, or roll up his eyes like a zombie. Then his father would give Buddy the camera, a heavy, expensive-feeling Canon with an adjustable lens, which his father always asked if Buddy knew how to use. Through its viewfinder, Buddy would try to compare the smile his father wore with Mary Winifreed to the one in his mother's photo album, and find he could not tell a difference. Sometimes, he jiggled the camera, or pulled the focus, to blur them. Then his father would replace his own camera in the leather bag, take Buddy's mother's camera from it, and give it to Mary Winifreed. Buddy and his father would pose as they had in the first picture. But before the shutter clicked, Buddy would close his eyes, so that his mother could not see into his soul. Now he was concerned, not about his soul, but that his father would find some way to deny him the camera.

Mary Winifreed placed her napkin over her food, which she'd barely touched, and said with false lightness, "Shall we take some pictures before the tour?"

"Buddy?" his father said. "Didn't you want to look at souvenirs?"

"Sir—" Buddy said.

His father's smile tightened, and his gaze shifted toward Mary Winifreed. Another unspoken rule was that Buddy couldn't ask about the camera in front of her.

In the gift shop, inflatable sharks drifted in air-conditioned currents, attached to the ceiling by nylon fishing wire. Rubber sharks, identical to one his mother had bought him to take to the beach long ago, were piled in plastic bins like corpses.

It seemed to Buddy that he had let his eyes off his father for only a second; but when he turned around, his father was not there. A fist tightened in his gut. He found Mary Winifreed pretending to interest herself in a display of porcelain thimbles. She regarded him wearily, her gray eyes sharper, her voice one she used when his father wasn't around.

"What's wrong with you two?" she said. "Maybe he's just gone to the trolley."

Through the gift shop's plate glass windows, Buddy scanned the milling crowd; people in shorts and T-shirts, fat and thin, young and old, were carrying yellow plastic shopping bags, eating cotton candy and hot dogs.

He started out the doors. Mary Winifreed called after him. As he cut through the crowd, the heat, smelling of sweat and suntan lotion and grease, closed over his face like a moist palm.

At first, he mistook his father's white dress shirt and gray slacks for a tour guide's. He stood next to what looked like a train of giant golf carts shaded with red-and-white striped canopies, which were also tinted with brown grime. When he saw Buddy, he raised his hand, as if he had been waiting for him all along.

A whistle blew, and the crowd began to stream toward the train of golf carts, blocking Buddy's path. A hand grasped his arm; Buddy tried to wriggle loose, but Mary

Winifreed held him. "I know you don't like me," she said. "But I've got to take care of you. Someday you'll see I'm on your side."

Buddy wrenched his arm from her. The crowd pushed them toward his father, who now stood on a trolley, looking down at them.

"All aboard," called a hatchet-faced young man, who wore a blazer with an official-looking patch. To Mary Winifreed, he said, "Please board, ma'am; you and your son."

"I'm not her son," Buddy said. "She kidnapped me."

Mary Winifreed glanced at Buddy, narrowing her eyes, then took his father's hand and climbed onto the trolley. Buddy sat on the other side of his father. His father grimaced at him, his face a mask behind which his pale blue eyes flickered with fear. Between them was the camera bag.

The trolley lurched forward. Over a bullhorn in a corner of the canopy, the guide asked how many people had seen *Jaws*. A polite smattering of applause answered him. "We've got Bruce," the guide said, "the mechanical shark, right here."

Mary Winifreed leaned forward, squinting at his father through a brittle smile. "Is something wrong, Jimmy?"

His father stared straight ahead. "It's nothing."

"Are you sure about that?"

His father didn't answer her. They entered a back lot where gaunt gray house fronts beetled over cobblestone streets; Europe, the guide said. Mary Winifreed turned to watch it. As quietly as he could, Buddy said, "Dad? You promised."

His father tilted his head and spoke out of the corner of his mouth, not looking at him. "I didn't promise you anything, Buddy."

"But, dad," Buddy said, more loudly. "I did everything you told me."

Beyond his father's profile, an American main street now passed, the gilt lettering on the facades' plate glass windows—a butcher's, a grocer's, a bank—superimposed on vacant fields. His father held his head rigid; the muscles in his jaw churned. "I never told you anything," he said in a dry whisper. "If you want that camera, you'll shut up."

"What is going on?" Mary Winifreed said.

Her face was a sallow blur. Buddy turned from her, wishing she would fall off the trolley and be run over by its wheels, one by one.

"What are you doing to him?" she said to his father.

"Nothing," his father said.

"It has to be something to have him upset like this."

"It's none of your business," Buddy said, hiding his face. "You don't matter. Me and him have got it all worked out."

"Buddy," his father said. "Don't talk to Mary like that."

But Mary Winifreed, in a calm, strained, patient voice, said, "What, Buddy? What have you and your father worked out?"

Buddy stared out of the trolley; gray buildings passed like an unfocused strip of film. Since they had left Colorado, he'd imagined his father would shoot her and dump her in the desert and they would become outlaws. But he couldn't say that; it wasn't true. A hot dry breeze blew into his face, and he held his stomach, thinking he would be sick.

The trolley locked into a track, and the familiar theme surged over the bullhorn. The guide announced that there had been reports of sharks.

"Buddy?" his father said. "Don't lie. I didn't promise you anything."

Whispers rippled through the crowd. Buddy wiped his eyes in time to see a sleek black fin cut through a lagoon. He felt his father lift the leather bag between them and smelled its cool dark scent as it was opened.

"Tell Mary the truth, Buddy," his father said. "And I'll let you have the camera."

The trolley crawled to a stop on a wooden bridge; the music shrieked and pounded. Slowly, Buddy turned to his father; the gaze which met him was hard and desperate, an outlaw's. Mary Winifreed watched him, her eyes flinty and sad. In his father's hands, the camera had become merely what it was: a black plastic rectangle, a cheap toy, almost nothing.

"Yes, sir," Buddy said, holding out his hand. "You didn't tell me anything."

Suddenly, the bridge tilted, sliding them across the plastic seat, pressing his father against his left arm, his right arm against metal railing. The crowd screamed as the music screamed. Bruce exploded from the water, chomping his jaws, thrashing his head, his movements supple and titanic, as if one of Buddy's drawings had come to life. Mary Winifreed shrieked, clutching her hands to her chest; even his father, still holding the camera, stared in mute amazement. Buddy reached out over the railing, trying to touch the shark, but his father grabbed his arm, pulling him back. Then Bruce changed, so subtly it was as if Buddy had glimpsed something out of the corner of his eye. From the shark he'd imagined, another shark emerged, teeth yellow, eyes dead black, jaws flapping, clumsily-hinged. His dorsal and medial fins were missing, chopped off to fit him into the pond; and beneath the water, Buddy saw, even more had vanished. A quicksilver chill spread through him, and a bitter taste flooded his throat. Struggling to break his father's grip, he bent over the railing, and vomited.

At the motel, Buddy lay on his bed, staring at cracks in the dim ceiling, listening to his father and Mary Winifreed's voices.

If he'd made a mistake, his father said, I'd have had to throw out that whole roll of film. What would I have told his mother? What did you tell her? Mary Winifreed said. I thought everything had changed before we left, and then when we were at your parents' place, I thought you didn't call her anymore because I was upset. His father said nothing, and the silence stretched out, a string about to snap. How am I supposed to keep waiting for you, when you used him like that? she said. How am I supposed to trust you? I never asked you to trust me, his father said. Then what am I supposed to do? she said. What's going to happen? Nothing, his father said. Nothing's going to happen.

Silence closed over the room like a held breath. His father's footfalls approached. Buddy shut his eyes. On his chest, he held his mother's camera, which Mary Winifreed had given him when he'd lain down. She had put her small, dry hand on his forehead, but he'd turned and shaken it off.

"Buddy?" his father said. "How're you feeling?"

"I don't know, sir."

"Do you feel good enough to call your mother?"

"No, sir," Buddy said. "I think I'd like to go home."

His father's weight settled on the bed. "Buddy? I'm sorry about what happened, but I'm in a lot of trouble now, more trouble than I was before. Will you look at me?"

Buddy lay rigid, eyes closed, gripping the camera. His father's rough, clean-smelling fingers hovered over his face. Tentatively, he touched Buddy's eyelids; Buddy jerked his head away, keeping his eyes shut tight. Using his hands as a vise, his father held his head, trying to pry open his eyelids with his thumbs, but Buddy thrashed from side to side. His father grazed his left eye. Buddy cried out, and his father let go.

In the next room, Mary Winifreed said, "What are you doing?"

"Nothing," his father said. He leaned close to Buddy. Buddy smelled the sharp scent of his aftershave, and the stale odor of his sweat, and felt his warm clean breath wash over his face. "Buddy?" he said. "I'm sorry. Will you look at me?"

"No, sir."

"Why not?" his father said.

"I don't know, sir. I can't."

After a moment, his father's weight rose from the bed, and his footfalls receded. In the next room, Mary

Winifreed asked how Buddy was feeling.

"He wants to go back to Houston. He wants me to call his mother."

"What are you going to tell her?"

"I'm going to tell her he caught the clap," his father said. "I'm going to tell her we picked up a bunch of hookers on Sunset Boulevard and he's indisposed."

"You don't have to be ugly," Mary Winifreed said.

"That's how it is," his father said. "That's how I am."

An outside door slammed. His father was gone. From the next room came Mary Winifreed's thin, frightened wails. Buddy felt his limbs tense, and his eyes begin to open; but he made himself lay still, his eyes shut, waiting.

If his father returned, Buddy knew, he might kill both him and Mary Winifreed. He might wake in the trunk of his father's car, bouncing down a washboard road. Then the car would stop, and sunlight would blind him, and his father would shove him into the desert. Buddy would walk tall, until the pistol crack, and darkness.

But that would not happen. He thought of what would happen. One Saturday, on the way home from the movies or possibly from Mary Winifreed's apartment, his father would stop at the photo store near his grandparents' house, where the plate glass door opened with a flat tinkle. His father would examine the pictures Mary Winifreed had taken with his mother's camera, then wipe his face with his hand and turn to Buddy, though he would not look at him.

Who took those pictures, Buddy? he would say.

Strangers, sir, Buddy would answer. Strangers took them.

Her brow knit, her eyes fierce, his mother would also search the pictures for clues. Each picture would be the same: his father and Buddy in identical poses, as if they had not gone anywhere, but stood in front of a blue screen. When she asked Buddy who took the pictures, he would repeat the answer he'd rehearsed. It would not matter whether she believed him; he had believed the pictures in her photo album, which now seemed to him as fanciful and suspect as stories of the Injun Chief and the Gray Ghost. Silence would descend between them. But eventually his silence, like Mary Winifreed's pictures, would tell his mother more than his lies.

What would happen when she knew? He could only imagine a kind of darkness, like darkness in which he now floated. He remembered his father's stories, and imagined, as he lay on the bed, the darkness at the bottom of the lake, where the dead soldiers lay.

In the darkness, the shark rose up, staring at him with a dead black eye; in it, Buddy glimpsed his own reflection, and felt brushed by something menacing and familiar. It resembled his father's tight grimace, and his herky-jerky gait; and in himself, Buddy recognized his own shrinking, his own cruelty, his own silence. Terrified, he opened his eyes, but they opened to darkness.

Little Deaths

He who finds his life shall lose it: and he who loses his life for my sake shall find it.

—Matthew 10:39

The air in my apartment was fetid, the heavy cloth curtains drawn, trapping the smells of cat piss and cat shit and something worse. I'd just gotten back from Houston and my head still felt painfully contracted, the black night air dense with threat. I opened the curtains, almost stepping on Monk, white in the darkness, who panted in the heat. Three white kittens suckled at her; another was stretched on its side, stiff, shrunken-looking, as if still feeding. Nearby, Lydia Lunch, the black kitten, struggled blindly, her eyes shut, mewling. I picked her up and tried to put her on one of Monk's teats, but she wouldn't take it. I held her cupped in my hands. Her heart hammered furiously, the beat of hummingbird's wings, so light that she was almost indistinguishable from the leaden air; yet each cool pad of her paws, each hair of her damp fur, each tiny claw, was distinct. I tried to remember, panic tightening like a band around my head, the dark panic rushing over my thoughts, how many days I'd been gone: two, three, I wasn't sure. I would find milk or water, feed her with a spoon, with the tip of my finger; she latched onto my thumb, her teeth translucent, needle-sharp.

By morning, another white kitten was dead. That left two white ones, and Lydia, who slept on my chest. As usual when I came back from Houston I hadn't slept but lain sweating on my bare mattress in a kind of waking trance: this time, a procession of corpses, human and otherwise, roasting in cold orange fire, crucified in Xes on metal frames, a vision that had no beginning and no end but seemed the revelation of a world truer than the one in which I lived. I looked outside at the shadow world, of trees and cars and neighbors walking past, horrifying in its certainty, and saw that the right front tire of my car was flat. I remembered driving on it, then I didn't, then I did. It was a mistake, I thought, that I was still alive.

Lydia Lunch slept, cupped on my chest, as light as air, as light as my soul. Monk, her mother, was the daughter of Henry Rollins and the first Lydia Lunch, my cats with Sarah, whom I had lived with three years before. Since I'd graduated that spring, I'd been going back and forth between Houston and my garage apartment in Austin, where I was now. A few weeks earlier, I'd noticed that Monk was pregnant. I'd come to the University as a National Merit Scholar, but now lived off my mother's credit card. I never visited my mother, because she reminded me both of my rotten childhood and my swiftly receding promise: my AP classes, my high school English honors, the expectation even by my family that I would become a writer. When I went to Houston, I stayed with friends I'd known since grammar school, drinking and hiding from the mess I'd made of my life. I had changed, my friends said; it was true. Since I'd lived with Sarah, my second year of college, I felt as if I'd misplaced some essential part of myself. I could not go a day without a drink. I thought the kittens would make me change, but now I understood that was a stupid idea. I wanted to call Sarah, to ask her what I should do, but it had been months since we'd talked. I could not call Sarah; I did not want her to see what I had done with my life.

I buried the two white kittens in the scrappy side-yard behind my apartment, then took the bus to the animal hospital near where Sarah and I had lived. There were other animal hospitals closer to where I lived in Hyde Park, but I didn't know how to get to them by bus. I would like to say that I felt empathy or sorrow for the kittens I'd buried, but I felt only shame. Already, I itched to return to Houston.

The old-fashioned University bus jounced and ground through gears, wind tearing through its open windows. When we first moved to the apartment, Sarah and I had ridden the bus, drunk as always, kissing hungrily, the dark air rushing around us, the bumps jolting our spines. Now Lydia panted in the breast pocket of my dirty button-down shirt. In my backpack, open on my lap, the two white kittens lay in the humid smell of erasers and pencil lead. The ancient driver, the same as when Sarah and I had ridden the bus, hunched over the steering wheel, his eyes two dark liquid slits, so that it seemed as if he were blind.

At the battleship-colored graduate student apartments, a family boarded, uniformly blond, their expressions earnest and smiling, their faces hardworking and shrewd, not much older, I thought, than Sarah and I, on their frugal way to some wholesome enjoyment I could not even imagine. Behind them, two blond-ringleted children dressed in white – and blue-striped railroad overalls peeked out, then shot up the aisle toward me before their parents could stop them.

"Is that a kitten in your pocket?" the tall girl said.

The smaller girl, rounder-faced, less innocent-seeming, tugged open my bag and looked inside. "What are you going to do with them?" she said.

My nerves jangled as if I'd been plugged into an electrical socket. My head felt freeze-dried into dust. I closed my eyes, trying to imagine a plausible answer.

"I'm going to help them," I said.

When I opened my eyes, the parents stood over me, staring, the mother tanned and flinty, capable, I imagined, of skinning a steer. Behind her, the father glared, square-jawed, fists clenched, clearly prepared to kick my ass.

"Is there a problem here?" the father said, with a slight German accent.

I could have told them about my car, or the cats'

sudden illness, or my own poverty, but I stared at them dumbly, imagining the tangle of athletic limbs that had produced the two blond carbon copies of them, their daughters.

"Don't worry," I said. "It's just a performance. Performance art."

The father grimaced. "Unethical," he said. "Sick."

The bus lurched forward. The mother, frowning, steered the girls, who were watching me, now, sternly, to a seat in front, where they turned like owls to look at me, before the mother pulled them back down, facing forward. The father still stood in the aisle, keeping watch on me, as if to prevent me from corrupting them further.

I got off at the last stop, the same as when Sarah and I had lived there – an ancient bench, wood carved with graffiti obliterated by other graffiti, cement so old it was worn down to pebbles inside. Across the street, the decaying mall and liquor store, its ether-smell of alcohol and cardboard and dust, a smell of oblivion, of death: Each cell in my body cried out for it, senseless, grinding need that obliterated time, that made each moment eternal; but I knew I wouldn't make it to the hospital if I stopped.

When I opened the door of the animal hospital, a flat bell tinkled and air conditioning and bleach and dog-smell enveloped me, and I felt relief from the heat outside so sharp I thought that I might weep. The waiting room was the same as when Sarah and I had adopted Lydia and Henry, as when we'd taken Monk there to get her shots: blond beaverboard walls, stacks of magazines, a bulletin board collaged with photos of cats and dogs. Facing me was a chest-high counter, and behind it, a door with a circular window, like the window of a ship, and behind the counter, a man who wore a small tidy gold hoop earring, who had also been there before.

The man looked up from a book.

"Can I help you?" the man said.

Behind me, a dog barked. In the far corner of the waiting room, a young woman my age—only an outline: blond hair, tanned legs—clutched a black dog on her lap. I knew how the man and young woman saw me: I wore tennis shoes and dark socks, a dirty dress shirt and khaki pants; I hadn't gotten a haircut in three years; I looked like a homeless person, but not a homeless person, and I knew that my indefiniteness was frightening and repellent, because it frightened and repelled me, too.

"Can I help you?" the man said.

In my backpack, the kittens plucked at the fabric, a sound like slow pattering rain. Behind me, the dog whined; for a moment, I thought the young woman would let it tear across the room at me, though at the same time, I knew this wasn't true.

"I used to live here," I said. "My girlfriend and I had some cats. The cats had a litter. One of the kittens had a litter, before I could get her fixed."

I didn't know why I told the man all this. I didn't know what I wanted from him. The man was older than I, a graduate student, an Austin type long since disappeared: clean white socks, jeans cut off just above his knees, a neat asymmetrical haircut. The man grinned at me, but I didn't know what it meant.

"Oh, yeah," the man said. "I remember you. You should really get the mother fixed. Too many strays in

Austin, as it is."

The man kept grinning, and I remembered how he'd examined Sarah and me, with curiosity and contempt.

"Where are the kitties?" the man said.

Going there, I thought, had been a mistake. When I tugged Lydia out of my pocket, she cried, digging her claws into my shirt, then my fingers, which were filthy and cigarette-stained; then she set out unsteadily across the counter, her head bobbing like a needle in a sewing machine, her eyes squeezed shut. The dog barked, and the woman shushed him. The man held out a finger for Lydia to sniff.

"How old are they?" he said.

It had been a week since Monk littered. I remembered how, when the first Lydia had Monk, Sarah had made a nest of old towels in an orange crate in our kitchen; the apartment smelled feral for months, before we could give the kittens away. I'd complained bitterly about the smell, but the kitchen had always been full of people, of life. I remembered how Sarah had filmed our friends' reactions with a Super-8 camera, the kittens who survived and the kitten who died, how Sarah had kept the camera running, trained on the kitten even as it struggled for breath. *Little Deaths*, she'd called the film. I didn't know now what the right answer was.

"A month," he said.

Behind me, the dog panted. Lydia clung like a black caterpillar to the man's pale finger, mouthing its tip. I wondered if the young woman could hear me and tell that I was lying.

"I can't help you," the man said. "They're too young.

They need to be weaned. You need to take them home."

I didn't answer him.

"How many others?" the man said.

"Two," I said.

"Three kittens then," the man said. "Let them nurse a few more weeks. Bring them back. We'll spay and neuter them, even the mother, no charge. We can give them away here, or you can put up a sign: Free Kittens. No problem."

Sweat trickled down my back, a sour inhuman chemical smell. My eye sockets felt lined with sandpaper, my throat parched so tight it might split like a dry husk, my head as if it might burst into a million dry wriggling fragments. I watched the man's pale, tapered, graceful fingers, wishing that they were my own.

"I can't," I said.

"Why not?" the man said.

"I just can't."

"Is there something wrong with the mother?" the man said. "You can feed them with an eye dropper. You can feed them with a baby bottle."

"I can't," I said.

The man looked at me. I knew he couldn't see the vision that played over my waking life, even now, like a superimposed film, the figures crucified in cold orange fire. The man could not feel my parched throat and sandpaper eyes and the pressure that mounted inside my head, threatening to tear it apart. I knew the man saw only my face, which I myself no longer looked at in mirrors, afraid I would see no reflection; but somehow, I thought, the man had seen inside me, even if he didn't like what he saw.

"Okay," the man said. "Wait here."

The man opened the door with the round window and it swung shut behind him. The book on the counter was a math textbook, its equations as meaningless to me as hieroglyphs. Lydia sniffed at the book. I could leave her and the other kittens there. The man would nurse them back to health, and they would become part of other people's lives. It would mean I would never be able to show them to Sarah, to prove I didn't kill everything I touched. In my backpack, the kittens plucked at the fabric. I could feel the young woman watching me. I didn't know what I should do. Beyond the door with the round window, I heard voices, coming to talk to me; I left the backpack with the kittens on the counter, and swept off Lydia, weightless, cupping her against my chest, and carried her out the front door, not looking at the young woman.

Outside, sunlight ricocheted off cars and plate glass windows and the rush of cars on the freeway and roar of a jet landing at the airport deafened me. Lydia cried, her heart pounding frantically, digging her claws into my chest. I knew I could not just stand there. I knew I should go back to the bus stop. I should call a cab from the pay phone outside the liquor store. I could put it on my mother's credit card. But even as I thought these things, I found myself walking, as if not I but someone else were walking, away from the bus stop and liquor store, toward the house where Sarah and I had lived.

Here were the apartments where curtains fluttered

through broken windows, and children ran, vanishing and reappearing. Here was the Carousel Lounge, crudely painted with circus scenes of acrobats and lion tamers, whose blank faces and blunted limbs had seemed to me terrifying and profound. Each Sunday, hulking cars lined the street, and old couples shuffled, leaning together like scarecrows, to disappear inside. Each day for a year, I had walked this street, going back and forth to the University, repeating to myself, like a mantra or a prayer, that I was a National Merit Scholar, that I had read T. S. Eliot and Søren Kierkegaard and Teilhard de Chardin, terrified I would vanish into what I saw; and now, walking down the street, I saw that the person who had thought these things, had vanished without a trace.

I remembered Sarah carrying her father's Air Force duffel bag, almost as large as she was, off the bus, carrying plastic milk cartons of sketchbooks and glass jars stained milky-white with paint, wearing her hand-dyed T-shirt and olive-drab men's shorts, determined to escape the dorm, to escape her broken family. We couldn't think about our childhoods, she'd said. To become artists—for her ambition, that year, had been to paint, and mine, to write—we had to forget about who we thought we were; we had to lose ourselves, to lose our minds.

The gray-shingled duplex was still there, where the street dead-ended at an orange- and-white-striped highway barrier; I looked up at the high, small second-story kitchen window whose screen still hung askew, at the boxlike screened-in porch that listed away from the house at the top of the stairs, looking for traces of who I had been when I was there, as if I could find myself there again. But the house, like the street, refused to give up its secrets: the crunch of my steps on the gravel driveway, the chicken wire fence around the back yard, the abandoned green car at the end of the driveway, now appeared to me in all their strangeness. I remembered how, on our first night there, we lay on a sleeping bag on the bare wooden floor, listening to gunshots or fireworks pop lazily in the vast darkness outside, how Sarah's hands were always stained with paint or ink, how they always made me think of sex, and not only of sex but something else, as if I could disappear inside her, as if in her I could find myself.

At the end of the gravel driveway was the creek, where we had gone when we first moved to the apartment, when we had done such things, gathering trinkets—tiny delicate animal skeletons, bits of colored glass, nameless parts of machines. I pushed through the thicket of bushes and vines, cupping my hand over Lydia in my pocket. The light turned green and cool, the coolness breathing up from the creek, the creek that wasn't a creek, just a ditch that ran behind the apartment complexes. A couch, a refrigerator, an axle, bags of garbage slid down the banks. My eyes throbbed, my vision dappled with after-images of light. One afternoon, one moment, one glance was still vivid. Sarah had turned to me, smiling, trusting me, a lightening glance; but I had not been equal to her trust in me, I had not been equal to my own hope for myself. That summer, I had tried to write, but found in myself a vast, terrifying silence.

A few weeks before we moved, we hosted the premiere of *Little Deaths*, projected on our living room wall. Our friends watched themselves, fussing over Lydia and Henry's kittens, or reacting to them with studied befuddlement, or using them as ironic props. But during the scene of the kitten's death, they fell silent, watching themselves. Their faces became at once older and more childlike, revealing who they had been and who they would become. I remembered how brutal I had thought Sarah had been to keep filming the kitten's death, how her brutality had frightened me; but as I looked from our friends' faces, shadows on the wall, to their faces, watching themselves, I'd known she had committed an act of brutal grace. And in the darkness, next to me, I saw that she wept, and knew that my fear had blinded me to who she had been.

At the bottom of the bank I crouched watching water flash over rock, catching sunlight, refracting, vanishing, before it was replaced—not replaced; entwined, overtaken—by the next vanishing gleam of sunlight moving ceaselessly through the rocks: even in this single moment, in this small place, a vast complexity of moments, all of them vanishing.

You are so afraid of the big deaths, Sarah had written to me one night when I was passed out. You kill yourself with little ones.

Lydia dangled in my front pocket. My shirt was wet with her urine, its stinging ammoniac smell. I didn't know what I should do. Each day since I'd lived with Sarah I had vowed to stop drinking, to change my life, and each day I had betrayed myself. I closed my eyes, hoping to be shown what I should do; but the desiccated crucified bodies cycled endlessly, senselessly banal, as banal as my fear, as banal as my grinding need for booze. I opened my eyes and lifted Lydia out of my pocket. Each tooth, each hair of her fur, each pad of her paws was distinct. Through her baggy skin I traced the string of vertebrae in her spine. She dug her teeth into the skin between my forefinger and thumb, her eyes still tightly shut. I dipped my hand in the water; she fussed, shaking water off her paws, refusing to drink. I imagined bringing her to Sarah; I couldn't. I imagined making a nest for Monk and Lydia, laying out bowls of food and water; I couldn't. I imagined cupping Lydia in my hands, closing my hands so she wouldn't struggle, holding her beneath the bright flashing stream.

But I could not do that, either. I rose, my legs stiff, and started back to the street, holding Lydia Lunch against my chest, knowing I had solved nothing, I had redeemed nothing; I knew it had nothing to do with me.

Acknowledgments

The stories in this book were written over a period of twenty years. They would not have been possible without the kindness, guidance, and patient support of many friends, teachers, and institutions:

I have been incredibly fortunate to have had many extraordinary teachers who have shaped these stories: Elizabeth Harris, Pamela Painter, Margot Livesey, James Carroll, Tobias Wolff, Elizabeth Tallent, and the great John L'Heureux.

My colleagues in the Wallace Stegner Program also left indelible marks on my work: Adam Johnson, Tom Kealey, Stephen Elliott, Eric Puchner, Malena Watrous, Katharine Noel, Lysley Tenorio, Jack Livings, Gabrielle Calvacoressi, Clementine Guirado, and Andrew Altschul.

I have also been lucky to receive support for my work from the following institutions: The Wallace Stegner

Program, the National Endowment for the Arts, the J. Frank Dobie Paisano Foundation, the MacDowell Colony, the Helene Wurlitzer Foundation, the Bread Loaf Writers' Conference, the Massachusetts Cultural Council, the Texas Institute of Letters, the St. Botolph Foundation, the Vermont Studio Center, the Grub Street Writers Workshops, the Lighthouse Writers Workshops, Writespace Houston, and Inprint Houston.

Thanks also to the editors who have given my work a home: C. Michael Curtis, Don Lee, Speer Morgan, Michael Koch, Robert Giron, Anthony Varallo, Toni Graham, Jodee Stanley, Rusty Barnes, and Rod Siino; and especially to the team at Texas Review Press who have given these stories a home and whose editorial insights have made them better: J. Bruce Fuller, PJ Carlisle, Karisma "Charlie" Tobin, and Megan McKinley.

To my friends and family, thank you for your patience, support, and love: Will Puryear, Burton Cleveland, Elizabeth Sacaris, Krista Kleypas, Karen Kelly, Herb Phelan, Patrick Delaune, Alexis Londo, Michele Cotton, Nancy Wiles, Stacey Burns, Steve Carson, Andrea Dupree, Ivan Gold, Shira Shaiman, Rishi Reddi, Daphne Kalotay, Julie Rold, Kate Wheeler, Jamie Portwood, Stephanie Reents, Sean McNeely, Caitlin McNeely, Cheryl McGrath, Alice Mayra McGrath, Lara Krepps, and Isobel and Calamity Farone.

Stories in this collection first appeared in the following magazines:

Crazyhorse, "No One's Trash," Number 95

Epoch: "Pictures of the Shark," Vol. 51, No. 3
"Little Deaths," Vol. 67, No. 2
"Ariel," Vol. 69, No. 3

Night Train: "King Elvis," Vol. 1, No. 1. Reprinted in *Night Train: The First Ten Years*

Ploughshares: "Tickle Torture," Vol. 27, No. 4

The Virginia Quarterly Review: "Snow, Houston, 1974," Vol. 78, No. 1.

In addition:"Pictures of the Shark" received special mention from *The Pushcart Prize XXVIII: Best of the Small Presses*, and "Tickle Torture" was shortlisted for *The O. Henry Prize Stories 2003,* and *The Best American Short Stories 2002.*

The author gratefully acknowledges permission to reprint verses from "The Drunken Boat," *Arthur Rimbaud: Complete Works,* translated from the French by Paul Schmidt. Copyright © 1967, 1970, 1971, 1972, 1975, by Paul Schmidt. Used by permission of HarperCollins Publishers.